Yahrah St. John is an international author of over twenty books, including several Harlequin Kimani Romance titles. St. John is the recipient of the 2013 RT Reviewers' Choice Best Book Award for Best Kimani Romance for *A Chance with You*. St. John has delivered numerous lectures at writing workshops and conferences nationwide. A graduate of Hyde Park Career Academy, she earned a Bachelor of Arts degree in English from Northwestern University. She discovered her love of writing at the tender age of twelve when she penned her first story. St. John is a member of Romance Writers of America, but is an avid reader of all genres. She enjoys the arts, cooking, traveling, basketball and adventure sports, but her true passion remains writing. St. John lives in sunny Orlando, The City Beautiful. For more information and author updates, please visit yahrahstjohn.com.

Books by Yahrah St. John

Harlequin Kimani Romance

Two to Tango
Need You Now
Lost Without You
Formula for Passion
Delicious Destiny
A Chance with You
Heat Wave of Desire
Cappuccino Kisses

Visit the Author Profile page at Harlequin.com

D1020966

To my love and friend, Freddie Blackman.

Cappuccino Kisses

YAHRAH ST. JOHN

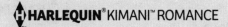
HARLEQUIN® KIMANI™ ROMANCE

Special thanks and acknowledgment are given to Yahrah Yisrael for her contribution to The Draysons: Sprinkled with Love.

Recycling programs
for this product may
not exist in your area.

ISBN-13: 978-0-373-86453-9

Cappuccino Kisses

Copyright © 2016 by Harlequin Books S.A.

For questions and comments about the quality of this book please contact us at CustomerService@Harlequin.com.

H HARLEQUIN®
™ www.Harlequin.com

Printed in U.S.A.

Chapter 1

"Welcome to the Lillian's of Seattle grand opening," Lillian Drayson, founder of the renowned Chicago bakery told the large crowd gathered in her second location. "We Draysons—" she turned to look at her grand-niece, Mariah, and grand-nephews Chase and Jackson "—are excited to open up this new bakery in the Denny Triangle section of town. It's a vibrant location with a plethora of professional and residential communities whose members will enjoy the delicious baked goods the Drayson family has been providing to the Chicago area for over forty years, and will now to the city of Seattle."

Applause erupted as the entire Seattle Drayson family cheered on Lillian, the matriarch, whose name they proudly represented at the new bakery.

Mariah Drayson stood away from the crowd and surveyed her family as she sampled one of the salted caramel cupcakes from the back of the room. She knew she shouldn't be eating another cupcake given that she'd already had one earlier that afternoon, but she had a tendency to eat when she was nervous. Opening her own bakery with her brothers was definitely something to make her worry. She'd used every penny of her divorce settlement from her ex-husband, Richard Hems, to cover her share, but deep down Mariah knew the venture would be worthwhile in the end. After the divorce, she'd chosen to go back to her maiden name. She was happy she did because Lillian's was a family business run by Draysons.

At age seventy-nine, her aunt Lillian was a force to be reckoned with, and when she'd decided to open a second location last summer, Mariah and her brothers had been initially reluctant. Mariah had been coming off the heels of a divorce and didn't know anything about running a bakery. Sure, she had a flair for baking after the summers she'd spent in Chicago learning at Lillian's knee, and during her self-imposed hiatus from work while she and her ex-husband had tried to become pregnant, but this was different.

Aunt Lillian would be entrusting her name, her brand, to the three of them. After much discussion, however, Mariah and her siblings had figured that each of them brought something different to the table. As well as being the best baker, she knew advertising and marketing. Chase, the numbers man, would keep track of the bakery's finances. Then there were was Jackson, bringing up the rear as a businessman and social media guru, and with a knack for cakes. Mariah smiled as she remembered how Lillian's of Seattle had been born.

The bakery was a labor of love for all of them, and they'd mutually agreed that Aunt Lillian should give the speech at the grand opening and ribbon cutting ceremony. It was her namesake, after all, and she was highly admired across the country after the Chicago Draysons had won the You Take the Cake competition three years ago on national television.

"Can you believe we did it, sis?" Jackson asked from her side.

Mariah hazarded a glance at her charming, handsome brother, who was two years her senior. Lillian's was the first time he'd actually stuck with a job longer than a few months. Though he'd done well at the private school all three siblings had attended, Jack was easily bored. He'd had numerous entrepreneurial successes, but as soon as they began to blossom, he would sell them. Would this time be any different? Mariah sure hoped so.

"No, I can't," she finally answered. After they'd found a location and Chase had worked out the finances, the bakery had come together, allowing them to open now, in early spring.

Jackson glanced her way. "Don't look so surprised, Mariah. With your baking skills, Chase's business acumen and my charm, we have what it takes to make this place a success." He swung his arms wide and motioned to the packed bakery, which was filled with family, friends, the news media and people who loved baked goodies. "We'll show them that we're as good as they are."

Mariah followed her brother's gaze and saw it resting on Belinda, Carter and Shari Drayson, their cousins from Chicago. "Why are you so mistrustful of them?"

"'Cause," Jackson said, "you know Grandpa Oscar always says they can't be trusted."

"We—" Mariah pointed between the two of them "—have no beef with our cousins. If Grandpa Oscar and Great-Uncle Henry have issues over money, that doesn't mean we should. Belinda, Shari and Carter have been nothing but gracious to us and have helped us in the kitchen."

The three had flown in from Chicago several days earlier to help make pies, cakes and tortes for the grand opening. They'd been in the kitchen baking and sweating as much as the rest of them. And Carter, being the skilled artisan cake maker he was, had created several works of art that were proudly displayed in their windows this very moment.

"That's because they probably thought we were inept," Jackson replied. "I mean, Shari's running Lillian's of Chicago. She probably wanted to make sure we weren't going to mess anything up that might get thrown back on her."

"Well, we didn't," Mariah stated. "And this is a success. Can't we just be happy today of all days?"

"Happy about what?" Chase came over and joined their huddle, wrapping his arms around their shoulders.

Mariah glanced up at her six-foot-four brother. He, too, was easy on the eyes, but in a studious way thanks to the wire-rimmed glasses, dress shirt and khaki pants he always wore while at the bakery. "We were just talking about what a great turnout this is, and I was reminding Jackson that we should be thankful so many people came out to support us."

"Yeah, I can't believe how packed it is," Chase commented. "It's a good start, but we put a lot of capital into the place and it's going to be a while before we see a return on our investment."

Mariah frowned. "Is money all you think about?"

"Yes." Jackson laughed and answered for him.

"Shh," Chase said, as a reporter posed a question to Aunt Lillian at the podium.

"Mrs. Drayson, coming into Seattle is a risky move for you, is it not?" the young Caucasian man asked, with a microphone pointed up at Aunt Lillian.

"How so?"

"Well, Sweetness Bakery has ruled the Seattle market for years," the man replied. "Other bakeries have tried to make inroads in the past and no one has been able to break into the market. What makes Lillian's any different?"

"Lillian's is different," she responded, "because we are a small family-owned business. I can promise the citizens of Seattle that they will enjoy the same high-quality baked goods as I make in my own kitchen, and that any customer would find in my flagship location on the Magnificent Mile in Chicago. That's what puts us a notch up over the rest."

Jackson stepped forward into the crowd and clapped loudly. "That about does it for the speeches, folks. Please come over and sample the delicious offerings we've laid out today, as I think our products will speak for themselves." He ushered everyone toward the tables.

"Well said, Jackson." Aunt Lillian gave him a wink as her husband, Great-Uncle Henry, helped her off the podium. "Come on over here. And Chase, Mariah, you come up here, too, for some photos." She beckoned them all forward.

Mariah smiled at the command in the older woman's voice. She placed the half-eaten cupcake on a nearby counter and blotted her mouth with a napkin. She wished she could touch up her lipstick, but had to comfort herself with the fact that at least she wouldn't have icing all over her mouth. "Coming…" She put on a bright smile and walked over in her brown peep-toe pumps toward the group.

After all the baking she'd done during the last three days, her smudged attire wouldn't do, so Mariah had gone home for a quick shower and change of clothes. She hadn't known what to wear for such a grand event and had erred on the side of chic elegance. She'd slid into a tailored denim pocket skirt and coral shirt teamed with a brown belt, and put a cream blazer over her outfit before rushing back to the bakery.

She'd arrived just in time to see her parents' noses wrinkle as they walked into bakery. Graham and Nadia Drayson were ultraconservative, especially her mother, and they didn't understand why she, Chase and Jackson had agreed to waste their money on such a foolish investment. Her father was a traditionalist who had made much of his sizable wealth in real estate, and fully expected one of her brothers to follow in his footsteps, but they'd chosen their own path.

Lillian's of Seattle wasn't some harebrained scheme. It was a family business, and with Aunt Lillian's seal of approval, they would steadily build on the brand. And why shouldn't they? Their cousins Carter and Drake, with their best friend, Malik, Belinda's husband, had already successfully branched off from the family business with their Brothers Who Bake blog and successful cookbooks. They'd even gone on tours and there was discussion of a potential television series.

Why shouldn't the Seattle Draysons get in on the action? When Mariah had presented the idea to Jackson, he was on board immediately. Chase had taken a little more convincing. He'd been working for a successful accounting firm and wasn't all that eager to give up that hefty paycheck, but eventually she and Jack had convinced him that with their aunt's support, it was a sound investment.

Mariah smiled as she, Lillian, Chase and Jackson posed for multiple pictures. Some were taken of them behind the display and a few others were outside in front of the stenciled Lillian's of Seattle sign. Mariah was trying her best to grin from ear to ear, even though her cheeks hurt, when she saw a sexy fine man strolling up the sidewalk toward them. He was clean-shaven, with a short haircut, and was nearly as tall as Chase. He wore a tailored gray suit with a checkered dress shirt and blue tie. Everything about him screamed money, which only enhanced his sex appeal. It was definitely the man who made the clothes, not the other way around.

Mariah didn't know who he was and wasn't altogether sure she wanted to, because the torrid sensations he was causing to flow through her body to the place between her thighs was making her feel flush all over.

He stopped when he reached them and paused for several seconds as he surveyed Mariah up and down, before opening the glass storefront door and walking inside Lillian's.

"Mariah!" Jackson called.

"What?" she asked, exasperated by the interruption.

"One more picture," the photographer said, when she turned back around after staring at the sexy stranger. Mariah forced herself to focus on the task at hand, and smiled buoyantly.

When the session was over, Jackson whispered in her ear as she quickly headed to the front door. "What's wrong with you?"

She glanced back at him. "Nothing. Why?"

"You just look funny, is all," he commented as he followed her inside.

"Well, I'm fine," Mariah replied. Or so she hoped. She glanced around the bakery for the mystery man. It was easy to find him in the crowd, because he commanded attention. She gulped. Her breath hitched and heart lurched into an excited rhythm. Damn! From across the room he was openly admiring her, and she didn't like the way he made her feel with just one hungry gaze. Her entire being yearned for something she couldn't quite name, didn't want to name. Why was this man having such a profound effect on her?

* * *

Everett Myers was intrigued. Not just by the new pastry shop that had just opened, but by the beautiful siren he'd seen standing outside by the sign. Who was she? And how could he meet her?

He'd come to find out if Lillian's was as good as the critics claimed, but as soon as he'd walked toward the group and photographer standing outside, he'd liked what he'd seen. Smooth caramel-toned skin, a pert little nose and straight honey-blond hair had Everett licking his lips. It wasn't as if she was dressed provocatively, either. She was stylish and classic in a cream blazer over a coral top, but it was the sexy blue jean skirt hugging her behind, allowing him to make out her curves, that had him standing at attention. She had to be in the neighborhood of mid-twenties, which suited him just fine. *God, what's wrong with me?* he wondered.

Deep down, he knew what. It had been a long time, too long, since he'd felt this way. Sure, she'd seen him when he approached, but since she'd reentered the establishment, she'd been doing her best to ignore him.

Everett wasn't used to being ignored. With him being six foot two, it was impossible not to see him coming. Plus, everyone in Seattle knew who he was. The Myers Hotel chain was synonymous with luxury and class, and had been a staple in the urban community for nearly thirty years. If people didn't know him personally, they knew of him or knew his name. He supposed that's why he was irked that the young woman who'd caught his eye was doing her best to feign ignorance at his blatant appreciation of her.

Just at that moment, the beautiful siren turned and glanced toward him. He flashed her a smile, but she quickly looked away. Damn, had he really lost his charm? He had been off the market the last nine years. He'd married Sara, his college sweetheart, when he was only twenty-one, and their son, Everett Jr.—EJ for short—was born soon after. But five years ago a tragic accident had taken Sara's life.

It wasn't easy being a widowed father at the grand old age of thirty, but he was doing his best to provide a loving, stable home for EJ. Up until now, he hadn't been eager to give EJ a new mom. Had he had opportunities? Heck, yeah! When he'd been single, Everett had often had women propositioning him, but as soon as he'd been widowed it got worse. They were all too eager to find out exactly how many zeros were in his bank account.

Or was he being too cynical? Maybe they just pitied him and felt his then three-year-old son needed a mother. And maybe EJ did back then, but Everett hadn't had it in him to even think about marrying again. He wasn't sure he could stand losing someone else he loved. And so he'd remained a bachelor the last five years, and quite frankly, had been content with the single life. Until now.

Determinedly, he strode over to where the gorgeous woman stood, speaking to a small group of people. She glanced up when he approached, but said nothing.

Instead, the man beside her, who had to be at least two inches taller than Everett, called out to him, "Everett Myers!" He held out his hand. "Pleasure to have you here."

Everett had no choice but to accept the fervent handshake. "And you are?"

"Chase Drayson," the tall man answered. "Part owner of Lillian's."

Everett caught the word *part* and looked the siren whom he'd fancied from across the room directly in the eye. Except now, standing so close to her, he found she was even more striking. "And you, would you be a part owner, as well?"

Her eyebrows furrowed. "Yes, but how could you tell?"

Everett inclined his head toward the door. "You were outside taking photos earlier, and I couldn't help but notice you."

His observation caused her to blush and she lowered her eyes, but that didn't stop the tall man from continuing the conversation, even though Everett wished he would go away and give them some privacy so he could get to know her better.

"We're all part owners," Chase offered. "Mariah, myself and our brother, Jackson, over there," He motioned to a man across the room surrounded by a group of young female customers sampling pastries from a platter he held.

"Mariah…" Everett let her name dangle on his lips. "It's nice to meet you." He offered her his hand.

Something shifted in the air between them. Something Everett hadn't felt in a long time. Awareness. Sexual awareness of another person, but not just *any* person. Her. It was several moments before she finally accepted his hand with a smile. "Pleasure to meet you."

A current of electricity passed between them at the slight touch, but then, as if Everett had imagined it, it was gone.

"What brings you by our little establishment?" Chase inquired.

Everett breathed in deeply. Clearly, her brother wasn't getting the hint that he wanted to be alone with his sister, so he needed to be blunt. "Perhaps I can explain to Mariah?" he asked, holding out his arm. "As she gives me a tour?"

Chase glanced at his sister and then back at Everett, and understanding finally dawned. "Oh, of course, I'll go mingle with the other guests. Have fun, sis." He gave her wink as he strode away.

Everett sighed. Thankfully, they were alone. "So—"

he grasped her delicate hand and slid it in the crook of his arm "—Mariah Drayson, what's your role here at Lillian's?" he asked, as she led him around the bakery.

When she glanced up at him with those brilliant brown eyes, Everett's stomach flip-flopped.

"I'm not only part owner, but head baker, as well." Mariah walked over to one of the tables holding a spread of pastries, muffins and scones. She reached for a petite orange scone and offered it to him.

"Really?" He arched an eyebrow as he accepted it. When he took a bite it was so moist and delicious, he couldn't help but groan out loud.

She blushed at his near-sexual response. "Does that surprise you?"

His brow furrowed. "Hmm. I guess so. You don't strike me as the domesticated type."

"That's because you don't know me," Mariah responded.

"I'd like to remedy that," Everett replied smoothly as he drew closer to her. "How about sharing a meal with me sometime?" Had he really just asked her out, with no preamble or finesse? He hoped she would say yes.

Chapter 2

Mariah coughed audibly. Had she heard him correctly? Had this impossibly gorgeous man with sexy dimples just asked her out? Her chest expanded as she responded to his close proximity. She could feel the heady attraction between them as her heart thumped loudly in her chest. It was as if he was magnetically pulling her toward him. "Excuse me?"

"You heard me," Everett said with a smile, as he reached for another piece of heaven on that platter. He popped it in his mouth and chewed as he watched her intently. He was clearly waiting on an answer.

"I—I can't," she finally answered. Awareness of him prickled across her skin and made her uncomfortable.

"Why not?"

"Are you always this persistent?"

"When someone is trying to avoid me, I am."

"And I'm trying to avoid you?"

He smiled. "You know you are. And there's no need. I don't bite."

Mariah wasn't so sure about that. Everett Myers looked like just the sort of man she should steer clear of. He radiated a sexual magnetism so potent that she shifted, restless on her feet.

"I'm waiting," he said, folding his arms across his amazingly broad chest. His voice was slow and seductive.

Mariah couldn't help but notice how defined he was. With his football player physique, he looked as if he spent a great amount of time at the gym, pumping iron. Everett Myers was sinfully sexy and he smelled equally divine. His cologne, spicy and woodsy, was tantalizing her senses, so much so that she had to step away.

"I've only been divorced a short time and I'm not ready to jump back into the dating pool."

His eyes followed her every movement. "That's too bad, but perhaps you'll change your mind."

"I doubt that."

"If you can't tell, I'm pretty persistent," Everett replied.

"I've noticed. You ran my poor brother off with that look you gave him."

Everett grinned unabashedly. "Did I? I just wanted some time alone with you."

"I'm sorry to have wasted your time, since I'm not on the market. But my pastries are," Mariah replied, "and you seem to like the scones. Can I get a variety box for you to take home? We have orange, lemon, triple berry and blueberry. Or perhaps something chocolate? Like an éclair?"

"Ah, the lady is changing the subject," Everett said, as she moved away from him toward the register.

She gave him her friendliest smile. "I'm starting a new business, Mr. Myers, and my focus has to be on making it a success."

He nodded. "I can appreciate that."

She frowned.

"No, I can," he declared. "Ensuring that my family's legacy continues is important to me, since my father left running the hotels to me."

"Omigod!" Mariah clapped her hand to her mouth. "You're Everett Myers."

He adjusted his tie and smiled with his eyes as she realized exactly who he was. "That's right."

"Of Myers Hotels," Mariah finished, as understanding dawned. "I'm sorry, I didn't realize…"

"Would that have changed your answer?"

"About?"

"Dating me?"

Mariah snorted. "No, it wouldn't."

He let out a full and masculine laugh. "I guess I'm a bit rusty, as I have been out of practice."

"Better luck next time."

He took a step backward. "Are you saying that I might have the opportunity to redeem myself and get another chance with you?"

"N-no. No." Mariah shook her head. "You misunderstood me."

"Did I?"

"Y-yes." She tucked her hair behind her ear. "Are you always this infuriating?"

"Only with you." He smiled.

Mariah let out a deep sigh. "You should really work on accepting the word *no*."

"Oh, I can," Everett said. "But I don't think that's why you turned me down."

"What do you mean?"

"I think you're afraid," he said, searching her eyes. "Because you felt the sparks between us as much as I did, but you're too afraid to act on it yet. And that's fine. I can wait. I'm a patient man when it comes to getting what I want."

"Why, of all the arrogant things—"

He pointed to the display. "I'll definitely have some of those delicious crumpets you fed me earlier."

He gave her a wink and Mariah's stomach lurched. Resisting Everett Myers was not going to be easy. But for her own peace of mind she knew she would have to, because her poor heart could not withstand being broken again.

After Everett Myers walked away with his box of pastries, Mariah was perplexed. How was it that he could sense her unease in such a short time? Usually she kept her emotions in check, so much so that even her family didn't know what was she thinking or feeling. Why? Because she was always looking out for their needs above her own. Even though she was the youngest, Mariah had always taken care of her older brothers. She'd been wired that way.

It had annoyed her ex-husband that she was so selfless. He'd always tell her to do more for herself, and she had. The one thing she'd always wanted was a baby. So when they'd had trouble conceiving early on in their marriage, she'd done everything in her power to ensure their success.

She'd spent three of the five years of their marriage in the pursuit of parenthood—a chase that went nowhere. At first she'd been unconcerned by her inability to conceive, but as each month passed, Mariah became further discouraged. When the doctor finally suggested aggressive fertility treatments, Rich hadn't been on board. He'd told Mariah he would be happy if it was just the two of them, but she'd always dreamed of motherhood and hadn't been willing to throw in the towel. The treatments caused a strain on her marriage, however, and Mariah didn't exactly help the situation by quitting her high-stress job for her phantom baby.

Instead, she'd watched everything she ate, even gave up caffeine and alcohol, as the doctors instructed. But nothing worked. Eventually Rich had had enough and told her their marriage was over. She'd thrown adoption on the table, but he had long ago given up on them, and they decided to separate amicably. Rich had even agreed to pay alimony, which had allowed Mariah to contribute her share of the bakery start-up.

"Mariah, there you are," Belinda Drayson-Jones said when she found her hiding behind the register. "You've been a hard woman to catch up with today."

"I'm sorry, cuz," Mariah said as she watched Everett interact with Chase, who couldn't resist stopping the hotelier before he could exit the bakery. Mariah was sure Chase was trying to pick his brain about some business deal, because her brother was all about the numbers.

Her cousin glanced behind her to find the object of Mariah's attention. "I'm not," she responded. "If that's who had you occupied."

Mariah blinked and returned her attention to Belinda. She was happy that her cousin had flown from Chicago for the grand opening of the bakery. They'd grown close during her marriage, when Mariah and Rich had lived in Chicago. "What did you say?"

Belinda chuckled. "Someone is sure infatuated. Who is that?"

"Just a guy who asked me out."

"Did he? And what was your answer?" she asked, leaning forward with eager interest.

"I told him no, of course," Mariah answered, stepping from behind the counter, even though she couldn't help hazarding a glance at Everett. When she did, she caught him staring at her, too, so she quickly looked away. "You know I'm not ready to jump into dating. It's only been a year since Rich and I separated."

"True," Belinda said. "But if you're honest with yourself, you'll admit your marriage was over well before then and was just limping along."

Mariah frowned deeply. "Thanks a lot, Belinda."

"I'm not trying to hurt you, baby girl." Her cousin reached for her hand and gave it a squeeze, "But you know I speak the truth."

"I suppose, but it's hard to hear nonetheless."

Belinda nodded. "I know. But it's time you start your life over, Mariah. You can't continue looking back at the past."

"How can I not, when my past could affect my future?" Mariah asked, as she watched Everett Myers leave Lillian's.

"Because marriages fail every day." Belinda fell silent for several long moments before saying. "Let me ask you something. Would you have left Rich if he hadn't left you?"

Mariah shook her head. "No, I wouldn't."

"Why?"

"Because I thought that if I just persevered for the both of us, it would get better."

"Did you ever think that perhaps Richard wasn't meant for you?"

"And he is?" Mariah pointed to the door Everett had just exited.

"No, but you have to get back on the horse eventually."

"That's easy for you to say," Mariah responded. "You're married to Malik and you guys are wonderful together."

"It didn't start out like that," Belinda said. "I fought my attraction to Malik, but in the end, I couldn't deny it."

"Yeah, well, there may have been some initial sparks

with Everett, but I need some time to sort through my feelings and my life without jumping back into the relationship foray."

"Who said anything about a relationship?" Belinda replied. "But a date is harmless. What could it hurt?"

Mariah rubbed her chin. A date with anyone other than alpha male Everett Myers might be harmless. But Mariah's sixth sense told her he would be anything but.

"Daddy, you're home!" EJ shouted when Everett stepped through the door of his penthouse apartment several hours later. Everett placed the box of scones from Lillian's on the side table.

"I'm sorry, Mr. Myers," his housekeeper said, rushing after the boy.

"It's okay, Margaret." He halted her, raising his hand. "You go on with your day while EJ and I catch up."

"Sure thing, Mr. Myers," the housekeeper said as she headed off toward the back of the apartment.

He lifted his eight-year-old son into his arms and ruffled his curly hair. He'd inherited the soft curls from his mother, along with that impish grin he was sporting right now. EJ reminded Everett of Sara, and it sometimes made him sad that she wasn't here to see their son grow up. Other times, it reminded him just how lucky he was.

"How's my boy?" Everett asked as he carried him to his study.

"I'm good," EJ answered, looking down at him.

"How was school?" He lowered EJ to the floor and then sat in his recliner to hear about his son's day, while EJ sat on the adjacent ottoman. It was their daily routine and a way for Everett to catch up on what happened.

"Fine, but I need you to sign off on a field trip." EJ produced a slip of paper from his back pocket.

"When's this?" Everett asked. Although he had a busy schedule as president of Myers Hotels and his own business, Myers Coffee Roasters, he made a point of attending EJ's field trips as a chaperone when his schedule permitted.

"At the end of the month."

"Sounds like fun. I'll be there."

"Aww, Dad," EJ sighed. "You don't have to come every time."

Everett frowned. "You don't want me to come?" He was crushed. He thought these were moments EJ would treasure, because Everett made time for him despite his busy schedule.

"It's not that…"

"Then what is it?"

EJ lowered his head and was silent.

"Well? I'm waiting."

His son's curly head popped up. "It's just that I don't want the other kids to think I'm uncool because my dad is a chaperone."

Everett smiled as he breathed a sigh of relief. He knew there would be a time when he would have to pump the brakes, pull back and not be so overprotective, but he'd thought that was a few years away. He was wrong. "If I promise to be a 'cool dad,' can I still come? What do you say?"

"Okay, but only if you promise not to embarrass me."

Everett chuckled as he held out his hand for a father-son handshake. "Sounds like a deal to me. By the way, I brought a treat for you."

"Oh, yeah? What'd you bring me?" EJ asked.

Everett rose from the recliner. "I'll be right back." He returned moments later holding the box of goodies from Lillian's. "I brought you these." He handed it to EJ. With the bakery's signature label on the top and the deliciously sweet aroma of fresh baked goodies emanating from within, he knew EJ would be in heaven.

His son's large, dark brown eyes opened wide with interest and he started to open the box, but Everett slapped his hand away.

"After dinner," he said. "Miss Margaret would kill me if I allowed you to eat that beforehand."

"Can't I have just one?" EJ gave him his best puppy dog look.

"Sorry, kid," Everett said. "That doesn't work on me, but good try. I promise we'll have them after dinner."

"All right," EJ replied. "How was your day, Dad?"

Everett was surprised sometimes when his son inquired after him. He was supposed to be the parent, not the other way around. But Everett suspected that EJ was curious why pretty much all he did was work, then come home most nights. Everett didn't have a social life to speak of.

Occasionally he went out on a date with someone his parents or friends fixed him up with, but most of those fizzled when the women realized he wasn't interested in marriage or commitment. They assumed he was in the market for a wife and mother for EJ, but were sorely disappointed by the end of the evening, or in some case by the second or third date, when they realized he wasn't budging.

It wasn't as if he was still mourning for Sara. He'd finally gotten over the tragic loss and had picked up the pieces of his life. He just hadn't been sure he was ready for another serious commitment, until today, when he'd seen Mariah Drayson. He wasn't sure why meeting the woman had him reevaluating his stance on marriage and commitment, but he was.

"Dad's day was good," Everett finally responded. "I

found that new bakery." He pointed to the box. "Has me thinking of new ideas."

"Like what?" EJ sat cross-legged on the ottoman and propped his head in his hands with rapt attention.

"Like expanding our coffee business at the bakery."

The idea had come to him almost immediately as he'd watched the large crowd at the bakery. What if he offered Myers coffee there for folks to buy along with their pastries? It would be a win-win for both firms, but especially Lillian's. Having the Myers brand for purchase on-site would only authenticate Lillian's promise that they offered the best and highest quality of products, given that Myers coffee was available only in high-end restaurants and coffee shops throughout Seattle.

"Sounds cool, Dad."

"Thanks, son." Everett smiled. "How about we get cleaned up and have some dinner?"

"Sounds like a plan."

Everett only hoped that Mariah and her brothers approved of his idea. It was good business and it would also give him the opportunity to spend some time with Mariah and get to know her better. He knew his play was somewhat obvious, but if she wouldn't agree to have dinner with him as a man, perhaps he could appeal to her as a business colleague. Time would tell.

"It was a wonderful turnout," Shari Drayson told Mariah after all the guests had gone and they were cleaning up after the grand opening. "I'm sure Lillian's of Seattle will be a great success."

"Thank you." Mariah smiled from ear to ear. It was great to hear such high praise from her cousin, given that Lillian had entrusted the flagship location to Shari several years ago. Mariah greatly respected Shari not only as baker, but as a businesswoman. When she'd lived in Chicago, Mariah had sat in on one of the family board meetings, and she could see it wasn't easy wrangling with all those personalities and big egos. But Shari did it with ease. Heck, she made it look simple, when Mariah knew it was the opposite.

Her cousin Belinda hadn't been happy with Lillian's decision for Shari to run Lillian's of Chicago. Mariah had always suspected that Belinda was Aunt Lillian's favorite because she'd followed behind their aunt when she was a child and was always in the bakery as her helper. And even though Mariah was closer in age to Shari, she'd always favored Belinda, who was several years older, and she'd wanted to be just like her. Belinda had a great sense of style, dressed in designer duds and never went out of the house without her makeup on. It also hadn't helped that Shari had gotten pregnant when she was in college, and had a son, Andre, while Mariah had been unable to conceive. Why was it so easy for some women to conceive without even trying, while she desperately wanted a baby and had struggled to get pregnant?

"Mariah?"

"Hmm…?" She drifted out of her reverie.

"I was asking about your parents," Shari said. "They didn't seem excited by the opening."

Mariah nodded. "They don't really support our endeavor, but that's fine. I intend to prove them wrong. Show them that Chase, Jackson and I have what it takes to get the job done."

"That's admirable," Shari said. "But I have to tell you it'll be a challenge, especially having two brothers involved."

"Because I'm a woman?" Mariah offered.

Shari nodded. "Sometimes it's hard for men to take direction from a woman."

"Was it like that for you in Chicago?"

Shari chuckled. "That and then some," she replied, "Everyone thought Carter, as the oldest grandchild, would have been chosen to run Lillian's, but instead Grandma picked me. Why? Because I have the business acumen, with my degree, and the creativity, thanks to the cake mix idea I came up with, to run the front of the house at Lillian's while Carter runs the back. And it's also why she chose you for the helm here."

Mariah smiled. "How do you manage running the front of the house and baking? Because you make it look easy." She'd already felt herself somewhat stressed at the prospect, even though she found it incredibly rewarding, more so than she ever had when she'd worked as an advertising executive.

"It's about balance," Shari said, "Trust me, it's not easy running the bakery business and being a wife and mother, especially now."

"Why now?" Mariah inquired. Unlike Jack, she had a healthy curiosity about her Chicago cousins and was eager to learn more about them.

Shari rubbed her stomach and then looked into Mariah's eyes with a huge grin, "Grant and I are expecting our second child. We're about to make Andre a big brother."

All the air in the room seemed to vanquish, as if sucked out by a backdraft in a fire, and Mariah thought she might expire on the spot. Not that she didn't wish Shari every happiness, but this was the last thing she wanted to hear.

Yet there was nothing she could do except stand there and fake a smile, because Shari was still speaking.

"We didn't want to announce it yet," she was saying,

"until I was in my second trimester, but I think it's safe now to tell the family."

Mariah pasted a smile onto her face even though deep down she knew it was less than genuine. She so desperately wanted to be in Shari's place, pregnant with her own child, but it wasn't in the cards for her. "That's wonderful, Shari. I'm very happy for you."

"Anyway, it looks like we're just about finished up here." Her cousin glanced around the nearly empty kitchen.

"Yes, it would appear that way," Mariah responded.

Carter had already quietly sneaked off, no doubt to call his wife, Lorraine Hawthorne-Hayes Drayson, who was at home with their twin boys in Chicago. Not only was Lorraine a twin herself, but apparently twins ran in her family. Given that Carter had been a committed bachelor, it had surprised the family when he'd wasted no time starting a family with the former debutante, whose career as one of Chicago's most sought-after artists allowed her to stay at home with their boys.

Mariah had hoped to spend more time with Belinda, but she had somehow disappeared, too. She was probably trying to catch Malik at the bakery, since he and her brother Drake were holding down the fort in Chicago.

"Let's get out of here." Mariah headed toward the door, with Shari on her heels, and turned off the lights.

As she locked up the bakery, it was hard for her to believe that she'd actually done it. She'd started her own business with her brothers' help. Now what?

Chapter 3

Mariah was the first to arrive at the bakery the next morning. Unlike Chase, who had a set morning routine of cardio and weight training, followed by a healthy breakfast, or Jackson, who was no doubt rolling out of bed late because he'd spent the night having too much fun with some unsuspecting female, Mariah didn't have any of those options. She was alone.

It wasn't that she liked it that way. She'd loved being married and all that it had meant. She'd loved being Mrs. Richard Hems and being part of a couple, a unit and a partnership. She'd always thought her marriage would last. How wrong she'd been, Mariah thought as she opened the back door of the bakery.

She couldn't focus on that now. She knew it wasn't healthy to keep looking back; she had to focus on other things. Namely, on baking all the breakfast goods that she hoped would be necessary for the morning rush. Aunt Lillian believed in providing the freshest baked products each day, so any unpurchased item was given away to a local shelter at the end of the night.

Mariah quickly turned on the lights, grabbed her apron hanging on a hook nearby, and headed toward the kitchen to get down to business.

Two hours later, she was wrist deep in flour when her brother Jack finally deigned to gift her with his presence. She'd already prepared the first batch of pastries, from cinnamon and pecan rolls to Danishes and croissants, for the breakfast rush. She was now starting on the triple berry, blueberry, lemon and orange scones that were a big part of their menu selection.

"Look who finally decided to join me," Mariah said, as he slowly made his way to the sink to wash his hands.

"Don't start, Ri," he replied, using his nickname for her. When he was finished, he grabbed a paper towel and dried his hands.

Mariah quirked her brow. "You were supposed to be here—" she glanced at her watch "—hours ago. I needed help. I haven't even started on the muffins yet."

"I'm sorry, okay?" Jackson responded as he quickly grabbed several mixing bowls and ingredients for the muffins from the cabinets and refrigerator.

She was surprised that for once he offered an apology instead of an excuse. "I presume you were with one of your admirers from the grand opening?" Mariah selected a handful of dough and set it on the already floured counter. She rolled the dough and used a scone cutter to cut out the pieces before placing them on a greased cookie sheet.

Jackson gave her a sly smile. "A gentleman never kisses and tells."

"Well, a certain gentleman needs to set his alarm so he's not late again. I can't do this without you," Mariah replied.

"Duly noted. What's got your panties in a twist?"

"Nothing."

Jackson stopped mixing the dry ingredients and looked at his sister.

Could he see that she hadn't really slept that well? The strain of the previous day had caught up to Mariah. She couldn't pinpoint exactly what had made her uneasy. Was it their parents' less than enthusiastic response to the bakery opening? Or perhaps it was meeting that sexy stranger who'd caught her eye from the second she'd seen him strolling down the sidewalk, and turning down his offer of a date? Or maybe it was Shari revealing that she was pregnant yet again, when Mariah's hopes of motherhood had been repeatedly dashed year after year during her five-year marriage? Maybe it was a combination of all three causing her lack of sleep. In any event, she'd been up with the roosters.

"You're frowning," Jackson said. "Did something happen last night? Did you go out with Everett Myers?"

Mariah spun around to face him. "Why would you ask such a thing?"

Her brother shrugged. "I don't know. Maybe 'cause the guy was really feeling you and cock-blocked anyone from getting close to you during the party."

Mariah chuckled. She hadn't realized that was what he was doing, but he had made his intentions clear, especially when he'd grasped her arm and damn near demanded she give him a tour of the bakery.

"C'mon," Jackson said, "I know it's been a long time since you've been on that horse—the dating horse, that is—but even you can recognize a man's interest in you." When she didn't respond right away, he asked, "Can't you?"

Mariah let out a long, exasperated sigh. "Of course I can. I'm not blind."

"Then why didn't you give the brother a chance?" Jackson inquired.

"I'm just not ready yet."

"Will you ever be?"

Luckily, Mariah didn't have to answer that question because the buzzer on the oven sounded, signaling that her second batch of pastries was ready. She scooted over to remove the delicious treats from the stove, effectively ending their conversation.

They didn't have a chance to pick up where they left off because their third baker arrived. Nancy Alvarez was a middle-aged woman with a background in the bakery business, and she knew her stuff. It had taken some convincing to talk Nancy into working for them, but once Mariah had sweetened the deal by making it part-time, with Mariah taking the early morning shift, she'd acquiesced.

Among the three of them, they were able to get a lot accomplished, and were ready to open their doors at 7:00 a.m. for the breakfast rush.

Since she'd been the first to arrive, Mariah left Jackson and Nancy in the kitchen while she attended to the front of the house. Customers slowly trickled in, wanting delicious baked goods, but eventually business took off and the morning sped by.

Mariah was surprised when Jackson came to relieve her for a short break, so she could get off her feet and have a cup of much-needed coffee.

Mariah went into the office and took a seat. She pulled off her comfortable flats and rubbed her aching arches. She hadn't truly realized just how exhausting running a bakery could be, affecting not just her sleeping routine, but her feet.

Owning and operating a bakery was hard work. The hours were long and the work tiring, but Mariah believed without risk there would be no reward.

Chase hadn't arrived yet. He typically didn't show up until 9:00 a.m., and Mariah envied his banker's hours from nine to five. He'd soon be scouring the pile of bills she'd seen sitting on his desk—invoices for the inventory of ingredients and equipment that it took to run Lillian's. Money was constantly going out and they would need to start pouring some back in to ensure the firm's viability.

She was leaning back in the chair, strategizing on an advertising campaign that would help boost business, when Jackson poked his head into the room. "You have a visitor."

"Who is it?" she asked, looking up, but he was already gone.

Mariah sighed. She didn't have time for visitors. She needed to come up with a plan to get Lillian's name out there. The reporter yesterday had been right when he'd indicated that Sweetness Bakery had a solid and long-standing reputation in Seattle and it would be hard to compete against them. But Mariah knew Lillian's recipes were superior and that eventually they would succeed.

Slipping her flats back on, she rose from her desk. After checking herself in the mirror that she'd installed in the office to ensure she would always be respectable before greeting the public, she headed out of the room.

When she made it to the storefront area, only a handful of customers were munching on their baked goods at the small countertop and bank of tables. Most were probably enjoying the free Wi-Fi Lillian's offered.

Jackson gave her a wink as he dealt with a customer at the register. "He's over there." Her brother inclined his head toward the far side of the store.

Mariah noticed a man kneeling in front of the display there, but she couldn't tell who it was. But as she approached and he rose to his feet, there was no mistaking the visitor's identity. It was none other than Everett Myers.

Fortifying herself and letting a rush of air out her lungs, Mariah walked toward the counter. "Good morning," she said with a smile. "May I help you?"

He returned the smile. "Good morning, Mariah."

"Mr. Myers, what can I get for you this morning?" she asked, purposely using his last name as she turned around. She grasped two plastic gloves and opened the display case.

He looked down at the pastries and then back up at her, penetrating her with his dark gaze. "Everything looks good."

The way he was gazing at her with such undisguised lust, Mariah doubted he was taking about the pastries. "Might I suggest the cheese Danish? We just baked them fresh."

"That would be lovely, but only if you join me?"

"Join you?" Mariah squeaked. Her voice sounded small even to her. "I couldn't possibly. In case you haven't noticed, I'm working."

"Looks like your brother has everything under control. What could it hurt to take a break and keep me company?"

He made it sound so simple that she should join him, and since resisting seemed only to incite his interest, as she'd learned yesterday, she said, "All right, but I can only spare a few minutes."

Everett glanced down at his watch. "A few minutes is all I have. And I will take your suggestion of a Danish along with a bottled water."

"Coming right up." She took a deep breath and reminded herself that Everett was just a man. But why did he have to look so darn handsome in his charcoal-gray suit and crisp white dress shirt that perfectly fit his athletic physique? Mariah could only wonder what lay beneath the clothes as she reached for the pastry and placed it on a glass plate, which was Lillian's signature. Aunt Lillian believed in serving people as if they were at her home, and not have them eat off paper or plastic. When she'd grasped a bottled water from the refrigerated case behind her, Mariah took the plate and mug to the table he'd secured.

She couldn't help but notice the smug smile Everett gave her as she left the display area, or the way his eyes roamed over her entire frame, taking her in from root to tip. "Here you are." She placed the items in front of him.

He rose to his feet. "Please have a seat." He pulled out a chair for her before resuming his own.

"Thank you," Mariah said, "So what brings you by, Mr. Myers?"

"Please call me Everett. All my friends do."

Mariah's brow rose a fraction. "And are we friends?"

"I certainly hope so," he answered, "If you hadn't noticed, I've been trying to remedy that."

Mariah couldn't resist a smile. "Yes, I have, and I appreciate the grand gesture of your stopping by, Mr.—Everett," she finally said. "But you needn't bother or try so hard. As I told you yesterday, I'm not interested in dating anyone right now."

"Does that mean you might be later?"

Mariah inwardly chuckled. Of course he would pick up on her word choice. "Later might be a long time coming."

"I can wait."

She placed both elbows on the table and steepled her fingers together as she watched him. "Am I a challenge to you, Everett?"

He didn't answer, because he'd chosen that moment to take a forkful of the Danish, and groaned aloud, causing a place deep inside Mariah to answer, just as it had yesterday. Her breasts tightened in response. She, or rather her body, was not immune to the virility of this man. "This is divine. Did you make it?"

Mariah flushed. "Yes, how did you know?"

He looked deep into her eyes. "I don't know. I guess that, because it was made with such love, I knew it had to be you."

Mariah swallowed hard and licked her lips. Everett's eyes followed her every movement and it made her uneasy that he was watching her so intently. "Um, I'm not sure what I'm supposed to say to that."

Everett took another forkful of pastry. "You don't have to say anything, since it's I who should be thanking you for the delicious start to my day. If you don't mind my asking, how did you get into baking?"

"I started baking in my tween years when I went to visit my aunt Lillian."

"Lillian Reynolds Drayson?"

"Yes, how did you—" Mariah stopped herself. Everett struck her as the type of man who never left anything to chance. If he wanted to know more about Aunt Lillian, he'd probably done his research. "Anyway, I used to visit her in Chicago during the summers and I would join her at the bakery. I learned the basics of how to bake at a young age. Once I grew older and was married, I had a lot of extra time on my hands and I began dabbling and trying new recipes."

"Your husband left you alone?" Everett sat back in his chair.

"It wasn't like that."

"No?" He quirked a brow as if he didn't quite believe her, but then shrugged. "If you were mine, you would only know one position and that's lying on your back."

Mariah flushed immediately at Everett's provocative statement. She'd never been so attracted to and aroused by another man before.

He gave her a mischievous grin. "Did I say something to offend your delicate sensibilities?"

"No, I'm just not used to men speaking to me like…" Mariah was at a loss for words.

"So openly about what they want?" he inquired. "I know what I want, and when I want something in life, I go for it with gusto, no holds barred. You get my drift?"

His eyes never left her face and Mariah was under no false illusion about what he meant. When Everett desired something or some*one*, he was fully committed. He was in. Mariah wondered what it would have been like if Richard had been like that in their marriage. Maybe if he'd been all in, their relationship wouldn't have ended and she wouldn't be divorced at twenty-six.

"Mariah?" Everett cocked his head to one side to peer at her questioningly. "Did I lose you?"

She blinked several times, bringing him and their conversation back into focus. "No, you didn't, but I really do have to get back to work."

"You're doing it again," he said.

"What's that?"

"Running away," he responded. "But lucky you, I like to chase." He rose from his seat, pulled several bills from his wallet and laid them on the table. He stepped toward her and Mariah was frozen, unsure of what to do. Was he going to make a move? Was he going to kiss her?

Instead, he just softly caressed her cheek with the palm of his hand, which was warm and tender, and said, "I'll see you soon."

And he was gone. Leaving Mariah to wonder and secretly hope when that might be.

* * *

Outside the bakery, Everett stared into the window at Mariah as she walked back toward the kitchen. What on earth had possessed him to come here just a day after she'd turned down a date with him? Although he'd dreamed of a certain beautiful honey blonde in his dreams, he certainly hadn't woken up this morning with the intention of acting on any of his desires. But somehow, as he'd exited the penthouse garage on his way to Myers Hotel, his car had taken him in a different direction, directly to Lillian's Bakery.

When he arrived, he'd thought about getting something to go, but on the other hand, he couldn't resist the pull he'd felt yesterday with Mariah. He'd wanted more. So he'd asked her brother to find her. And when she'd come out to the storefront, she'd looked just as sexy and scrumptious as he remembered. Sure, she was wearing a less than flattering apron that covered all her God-given assets. That was why he'd asked her to come around from the display—so he could take another real good look at her. Perhaps he'd hyped her up in his dreams to be more than she was, and reality would be like a cold splash of water in his face. But he hadn't been wrong.

Instead, when she'd come from behind the counter wearing low-rise jeans that sat seductively over her hips and a crop top that gave him just a hint of stomach and skin, Everett had been eager to know what secrets lay hidden beneath them. It hadn't helped that her full, round breasts were pressing against the thin top she wore, showing him that she might be a bit chilled.

Jeez. He glanced down at his watch and realized he'd better get to the hotel so he could make the morning's meeting, rather than stew over a baker who, if she had her way, could take him or leave him. Everett quickly drove the short distance to the hotel.

As he did, he realized he hadn't expected the full force of Mariah's sexiness to hit him with such magnitude as it had that morning, but he'd felt it deep in his groin. He'd had a hard-on happening when she hadn't so much as touched him. Matter-of-fact, she'd tried her best to keep him at bay throughout their interlude. That is, until he'd stuck his foot in his mouth and revealed exactly where she'd be if she were his woman. She'd be on her back in his bed and he'd ravish her all night long until she begged him to come inside her.

When had he gotten so horny? It hadn't been that long since he'd been with a woman, had it? Everett pondered the thought as he rode the elevator up to the administrative offices of Myers Hotels. Walking through the lobby had been a blur. As the doors opened, he blinked to get himself back in the game and on his morning routine.

The meeting was already under way when he arrived, and Everett merely stood back against the door, listening as the hotel's general manager went over the day's events.

When he was done, he glanced up and saw Everett. "Mr. Myers, is there anything you'd like to add?"

Everett shook his head. "Not at all, you go ahead. I'll just listen in."

Thankfully, the hotel pretty much ran itself, with Everett stepping in only periodically, when a major decision needed to be made. Hiring the best and brightest in the hospitality industry and paying them a fair wage had ensured that Myers Hotels were respected in the industry and one of the more sought after places of employment in the Seattle hotel market.

He slipped out before the meeting concluded and headed to his office. His executive assistant, Mildred, was waiting for him with his messages. There were the usual suspects, along with a message from EJ's school.

Everett immediately thanked Mildred for the update and closed the door to his office. Being a father came first, before business. It had been that way with his own dad and Everett was ensuring he did the same. Although Stephen Myers was a serious and austere man to some, he had always made sure that Everett and his mother were his top priority. Even when his father had been building the Myers Hotels into a well-respected luxury chain, he'd made certain he had time for his family. If ever Everett had a problem, his father had always been there to help him solve it. It was because of him that Everett was the man he was today. And it's why he'd wanted to emulate him by marrying his first love. He'd thought he and Sara would be together forever, until fate struck.

Everett picked up the receiver and dialed the principal of EJ's school, who'd left the message for him.

"Mr. Myers, thank you so much for the quick response," the woman said.

"When it comes my son, nothing is more important," Everett replied. "What's going on?"

"Well, EJ was having a hard time today, so I brought him to my office."

"Why?" Everett sat upright in his chair. "Is something wrong? Is my son okay?" Ever since Sara's death, he had become somewhat paranoid and hypervigilant about EJ's safety, but how could he not? EJ was all he had left.

"He's fine, he's fine. Physically, that is."

Everett understood her meaning. "And emotionally?"

"I learned there were some students picking on him…" She paused. "Because his mother is gone."

"I see." Everett's voice was clipped.

"I've disciplined them accordingly," the principal continued, "but EJ was clearly upset, as he has every right to be, and I just thought that—"

"I'll be there in twenty," Everett said, and hung up the phone. He grabbed his keys and sunglasses as he headed for the doorway.

"Is everything okay, Mr. Myers?" Mildred asked in obvious concern, since he'd only just arrived.

"It's EJ." And with those words, he was out the door.

He made it to the school in fifteen minutes, parking his car in the tow-away zone. No one would dare tow his vehicle, given the thousands he'd donated to this private school.

The look on his face must have said it all, because the receptionist rose as he walked straight past the front counter and toward the principal's office. He knocked twice and didn't wait for a response before entering.

"Mr. Myers!" The principal jumped up from her desk.

"I'm here to pick up my son."

He glanced across the room and saw EJ sitting at a table, while the principal looked up, startled, from her computer.

"Of course, of course." She rushed toward him. "And I'm sorry to have to bother you," she said, closing the door behind him so they could speak in private. "Just given the time of year, with Mother's Day coming in May, I thought it prudent you come."

"Thank you for calling me."

"You're most certainly welcome." She touched his arm. "And I can assure you that we don't tolerate bullying of any kind. The children have been reprimanded and their parents were contacted."

"I appreciate that," Everett said. "EJ, grab your things," he told his son over her shoulder, since he was several inches taller. He bent down to whisper in the principal's ear in a lethal tone, "Let's ensure this doesn't happen again."

The woman nodded.

Once they were outside the school, Everett stopped and turned to his son. "How you doing, buddy?"

EJ just he kept walking toward the car. Everett understood the cue that he didn't want to talk here, so he unlocked the Cadillac Escalade and EJ jumped into the passenger seat.

Everett came around to the driver's side. He turned on the engine, but thought better of it and said, "Do you want to talk about it now?"

"Can't we just go?"

"Not when something's on your mind," Everett responded. "You know you can talk to me about anything and I will always sympathize and be here to listen."

EJ turned to face the window and said nothing.

Everett sighed as he put the Escalade in gear. "All right. Well, when you want to talk about it, I'm here for you, okay?"

EJ didn't answer; he just nodded his head.

Chapter 4

Everett wasn't surprised when EJ claimed he was sick the following morning. Everett suspected it was a ruse, and normally would have made him go to school and face his bullies, because that's what a father taught his son. But in this instance, Everett couldn't make the boy do so, not when he knew this hurt went deeper because it was over the loss of his mother. He went to work instead, leaving EJ with Margaret, who'd keep any eye on him until Everett returned later that afternoon. He would make it an early day, so he could spend some time with his son.

But first he had a strong desire for another one of Lillian's pastries, or so he told himself as he walked toward the bakery. He opened the front door with a flourish and a bell signaled his arrival.

Everett was happy to find Mariah at the front counter instead of Jackson. "Good morning," he said, strolling toward her.

She sighed in apparent exasperation at seeing him for the second day in a row. "Everett."

"You're looking lovely today," he said, admiring the way her glorious honey-blond hair hung in soft waves to her shoulders. She'd clearly done something different with the style, but he didn't care. It just made her look all the more attractive to him. He'd love to rake his hands through it as he brought her mouth closer to his.

He liked everything about Mariah, from the color of her eyes, which reminded him of sandalwood, to her delicate round little nose, to the sinful curve of her alluring lips. Lips that he would love to kiss, tease and suck into his mouth.

"Everett?" Mariah was saying his name again and he had to stop staring at her as if she were a fresh piece of meat.

"Yes?"

"I asked you what you would like," she said, looking at him strangely.

"If I said you, would that be too much?"

She grinned at his come-on. "Are you always this much of a flirt?"

"Only with you."

"I'm flattered, really," she said, as the chime of the doorbell indicated another customer had just entered the bakery, "but as I told you before—"

"You're not interested," he stated, cutting her off.

She pointed her index finger at him. "See, you really are as smart as the internet says."

"Have you been looking me up?" Everett was intrigued as the familiar air of electricity he felt on the prior occasions with Mariah sizzled between them. There was no mistaking it. She was not as immune to his charms as she was leading him to believe.

Mariah flushed and he could see he was right.

"There's a line forming," she said, as yet another customer came through the bakery door. "What can I get you?"

"If you're not on the menu, then I guess I'll have to settle for one of those," Everett responded, pointing to the assortment of quiches they'd prepared as a breakfast selection. "And another of those scones from yesterday." He would bring a treat home to EJ in the hopes that it would cheer him up.

Mariah smiled. "Excellent choice." She opened the display case to procure his items. Once she'd rung them up, she said, "Have a great day and see you soon."

His brow rose a fraction. "Would you like to? See me, that is?"

"I always like paying customers."

He laughed as he made his way out the door. Mariah might be telling him to go away, but he suspected she was starting to enjoy seeing him come around just as much as he was enjoying seeing her each day. And if he had his way, it wouldn't be long before the walls she had erected around her would come tumbling down.

Mariah was grateful when she saw the back of Everett's head as he left the bakery. Today made the third time she'd seen him in as many days. She'd told him in no uncertain terms that she wasn't interested in dating him, but he kept coming back. The man was relentless and she wasn't sure how long she could keep turning him down, when it would just make more sense to go out with him and put him out of his misery. Maybe then he would see that they weren't a match and she was completely out of his league.

Everett was handsome and, according to everything she'd read online, wealthy as sin. Despite herself, she'd been unable to contain her curiosity about the man after he'd visited the bakery twice, and she'd tried to absorb as much information as possible on the man. She'd learned via an internet search about the accidental death of his wife, Sara. But the details were vague because Everett had secluded himself, keeping out of the news, pretty much right after the accident.

According to sources, he was currently single and had been that way since becoming widowed. So what could he possibly see in a newly divorced baker from an upper-middle-class family? For some reason Mariah presented a challenge to him, but perhaps as soon as he won he'd stop his pursuit of her.

"Was that Myers again?" Jackson inquired, coming up behind her and heading to the second register. He turned to the next customer in line. "Can I help you?" he asked.

"It was," Mariah said, as she smiled and handed her customer some change.

"Wow! Someone's sprung on you," Jackson said, after he'd fished out several pastries and boxed them up for his customer. "Here you go. Have a nice day."

Several minutes later, the storefront was empty and it was just the two of them, so Mariah turned to glare at her brother. "It's not that serious."

"Apparently it is for him," Jackson retorted. "He's been here three days straight."

"You can't count the opening, because he just met me," Mariah responded, reaching for a cloth underneath the register to wipe down the counter.

"I sure as hell can. The man was enthralled with you. Trust me, I know when a guy is interested."

Mariah laughed. "I guess it would take one to know one." She bumped his hip and continued wiping the displays.

"So what are you going to do about it?" He folded his arms across his chest.

"Nothing. Eventually, he'll tire of the rejections and move on."

"Ha!" Jackson laughed as he headed back to the kitchen. "You don't know men at all."

Mariah thought about her brother's words later that evening in her apartment, when she was cuddled with a bowl of popcorn, watching a romantic comedy. Jackson had been right that she didn't know men at all. Her experience with the opposite sex was limited to her college career before she'd met Rich, and there hadn't been much to speak of. She'd always been into her studies, leaving very little time for dating.

Now she had a rich, successful businessman like Everett Myers interested in her and all she could do was run. Mariah wasn't proud of it. She'd always prided herself on being a person who persevered even when things got difficult, as she had with her inability to conceive. She'd been the one who'd dug in the trenches, refusing to give up on her marriage even though she suspected Rich had checked out. Mariah had thought that she could win him back somehow and that in time he'd see that she'd done all of it for them, but he hadn't.

Mariah considered it one of her greatest failures. It was why she was reluctant to go down that path again so soon with Everett, even though she found him stunningly gorgeous. Every time he came into the bakery, Mariah caught herself holding her breath, and when he touched her, her entire body came alive. It made her feel things she hadn't felt in a long time, such as desire and passion. Whenever he was near, her skin became prickly and the place between her legs became heated. She wanted to push the feelings away, but Everett wouldn't let up. And did she really want him to? Of one thing she was sure—Everett could quench all her desires.

If he continued his quest of stopping by the bakery, Mariah wasn't sure just how long she could hold out before she finally gave in.

Later that afternoon, Everett returned to his penthouse and found EJ sitting at the breakfast counter eating one of the pastries he'd brought from Lillian's yesterday, while Margaret was at the stove, no doubt starting supper. Everett chuckled inwardly. Clearly, the boy wasn't that sick if he could enjoy the delicious concoction.

"Looks like someone's feeling better," Everett said, placing his briefcase on the counter.

EJ smiled and looked up, his face smeared with chocolate. Everett reached for a paper towel and threw it at him. "Wipe your face," he said with a laugh. "You have chocolate all over it."

"This is good, Dad," EJ replied, after wiping his mouth. "Where'd you get it?" After dinner last night, they'd been too full for dessert.

"Lillian's. And I brought another." He held up the box from that morning.

EJ reached for it. "I'll take it."

"Not before dinner, you won't."

"I was telling him the same thing, Mr. Myers, but he insisted on eating that one." Margaret gestured to the empty saucer in front of EJ.

"You'd better listen to Miss Margaret," Everett chided, pointing his finger in EJ's direction. "Don't you give her no sass."

EJ frowned. "I wasn't."

Everett loosened his tie and undid the top button of his shirt as he headed for the refrigerator. He took a bottle of beer out and quickly dispensed with the top before taking a generous swig.

"Why don't you come talk to me?" he suggested as he walked to the living room. "While Margaret finishes up dinner."

He heard an audible sigh, but EJ slipped off the bar stool where he'd been sitting and joined Everett as he settled on the couch. "So are you finally ready to talk to me about what happened yesterday?"

EJ shook his head., "No, but I guess you're going to make me?"

"Something like that."

EJ sunk deeper into the sofa cushions and was quiet for several long moments before he finally spoke. "There were some kids razzing me because I don't have a mother."

Everett frowned and sat upright. He hated hearing EJ talk like that. "You had a mother, EJ. Her name was Sara. She's not here with us now, but she loved you very much." It was important to Everett that EJ remembered her and knew that he'd been loved and was a product of that love.

"I know that, Dad, but I still don't like hearing about it. Have kids bring it up like I'm some sort of freak or something."

"You're not a freak." Everett patted EJ's thigh. "You're just different. And you have to be okay with that. You still have me, or am I chopped liver or something?" It was one of things he worried about—that somehow he wouldn't be enough for his son. Lord knows, he'd tried to be a father and a mother all rolled into one, but it was hard sometimes.

EJ gave him a reluctant half smile. "No, but it's...it's just not the same."

Everett wasted no time pulling his son into a firm hug and holding him close to his chest. "I know that," he said, leaning back to look at him. "And I know that I can't be your mom, but I promise you I will do my best to be both a mother and father to you. Whatever you need, I'm here." He gazed into EJ's dark eyes, which were cloudy with unshed tears, then tugged him back into his arms. "I'm always here."

"Love you, Daddy," EJ whispered into his chest.

Those three words were all that Everett would ever need.

Mariah stared at her reflection in the mirror in the bathroom of her two-bedroom apartment. She looked pretty darn good if she did say so herself. She was wearing her favorite pair of skinny jeans, a floral tunic and a long dangling necklace. She'd applied a trace of mineral foundation, mascara, and the finishing touch was lipstick. She typically never went to such trouble dressing each morning, since she spent the first few hours of her day in the kitchen. But the thought that Everett might show up again today had her making a special effort. Her stomach was in knots with eager anticipation of his arrival.

She must have been noticeably antsy because later that morning Jackson commented as much. "What's got you so jumpy?" he asked. "Every time the doorbell chimes, I can see you perk up. Are you waiting for someone?" One of his eyebrows rose with amusement. He knew the answer.

"No."

"Liar." He laughed as he continued with the fondant cake he was working on for an upcoming wedding. Jackson had become quite the cake aficionado and they'd already received a few orders.

"Am not."

"You're wearing makeup. And you're dressed up today." He eyed her attire and face before returning to his task.

Mariah glanced down at her outfit. She'd gone for casual chic, so as not to look as if she was *trying* to attract a certain person's attention or advances.

"C'mon, sis, I know you, and you can't get anything by me."

Mariah rolled her eyes and sauntered out of the kitchen. "Whatever." There was no denying that Jackson was right, but that wasn't what irked her. It was Everett. He was late. He usually came around 9:00 a.m. and it was after ten, which meant she'd gone through all this trouble for nothing.

She shouldn't be surprised that he'd finally taken the hint. She had given him the brush-off three times and he must have figured three strikes and he was out. She'd blown it.

The doorbell chimed and Mariah didn't bother looking up this time, so was surprised when she finally did and found his dark brown eyes looking at her.

"Everett." She swallowed the lump that suddenly formed by having the businessman yet again in her crosshairs.

"Hey." He smiled, showing off his sparkling white teeth.

"Hi." Mariah didn't know why she couldn't think of anything but a one-syllable word, and her heart was hammering in her chest.

"Surprised to see me?"

"Actually, no, I'm not," she replied, finding her voice. "You've been persistent, so I doubted today would be any different."

"Is that why you dressed up for me today?" Everett asked, raking every inch of her figure with his magnetic gaze.

Mariah started to say no, but knew it would be a bold-faced lie, so she led with the truth. "What if I did?"

Everett's eyes darkened and his expression shifted from flirtatious to something different, something she didn't recognize but knew to be dangerous. "Come from behind the counter and I'll show you."

Mariah wasn't sure she wanted to leave the safety that the counter provided. Everett looked as if he was ready to pounce and she wasn't certain she could or *would* fight him off.

"Mariah." He said her name again and it sounded silky and seductive coming from his lips.

She instinctively obeyed, ignoring the warning signals going off in her brain to beware. When she rounded the corner of the counter, Everett captured her hand and brought her forward until she was inches from his face, from his lips. Sensuously full lips that she had a hard time not focusing on.

"I'm glad you've come around to seeing things my way," he said, as his large hands skimmed over her forearms.

"Did I have much choice?"

He chuckled. "No, I didn't plan on giving up. But I have to admit that I didn't come here solely to see you."

"No?" She tried not to appear offended by the comment.

"Don't look so crestfallen," he said, caressing her chin with the pad of his thumb. "I have a business offer for you."

Why did he have to keep touching her? It was scrambling her brain and she couldn't think straight. "B-business? What business would you and I have?"

"That's what I would like to discuss with you, over lunch if you're free."

Mariah glanced behind her toward the kitchen. "I don't know. I haven't left the bakery since we opened."

"Can't your brother manage things in your absence for an hour or so?"

She blinked rapidly. "I—I suppose."

"Good." Everett obviously considered the topic closed. "Grab your purse."

"I didn't say I would go." She stood rooted to the spot.

He cocked a brow. "Are we really going to act like you weren't waiting for my arrival? If so, we can go back to your administrative offices, where we'd have some privacy, and see if that holds true."

The thought made Mariah warm all over, and nervous at the prospect of being alone with such a virile man, so she took the former option. "Uh—that won't be necessary. Let me just let Jack know, and I'll get my purse."

Several minutes later, she was sliding into Everett's Escalade as he buckled himself into the driver's seat. "I figured we could go to the Myers Hotel. There's a great restaurant and we can get in and out within the hour."

Mariah smiled. "Okay, thank you." She appreciated his thoughtfulness. But that didn't mean she wasn't nervous as hell being in the car alone with the man. A man she had secretly wished for, but still was uneasy being around. She couldn't explain the effect Everett had on her, but she felt entirely out of sorts. Her heart was thumping loudly in her chest and her pulse was beating erratically. So she tried to focus on something else. "So what kind of business offer did you want to discuss?"

"There will be time for that later," Everett said, looking over at her. "I'd rather know if this will be a one-time event, or will I see you again?"

"That's debatable."

"Then I'll just have to try my best to convince you."

They made it to the Myers Hotel in less than half an hour, and as he'd promised, the maître d' sat them immediately in a private corner booth.

"Thank you, Jacques." Everett said.

"You're most welcome, sir. Enjoy your lunch."

Mariah noticed the way the man showed Everett such deference. "Is it always like that everywhere you go?"

He shrugged. "Not always."

They perused their menus and in no time a waitress materialized to take their drink and lunch orders.

"What's it like to grow up with all this?" Mariah asked, motioning to the opulent decor of the restaurant on the fortieth floor, the windows of which overlooked the bay.

"It wasn't like this always."

"No?"

"No," he stated emphatically. "My father started this company from nothing. He only had the one hotel, which he and my mother put all their savings into. Luckily, with the right investments and partnerships, he was able to make it grow into a chain."

"Which you've taken a step further with your Myers Coffee Roasters importing business and coffeehouses in downtown Seattle."

Everett smiled. "So you really have done your research."

"It always best to know one's opponent."

"I hope that's not how you see me," he said softly, searching her face. "As an opponent."

"How would you like me to see you? As a potential love interest?"

"In time, yes," he responded, his gaze unwavering. "But as I told you, I'm a patient man. I can wait. That which cometh easily, can be easily lost."

Mariah nodded. "So why have you never opened coffeehouses nationwide?"

Everett sat back and stared at Mariah as the waitress returned with their drinks. He noticed how she'd deftly changed the subject to a more acceptable topic. Clearly, his interest in her made her uncomfortable, but at least she wasn't completely retreating as she'd done several days ago. She was slowly giving him an inch and he would take it and then some, but slowly, ever so slowly. His instincts told him that Mariah had been hurt before, which was why she was so cautious. He would have to take his time with her. Woo her.

"I didn't want another large chain," Everett said, finally answering her. "I wanted Myers Coffee Roasters to be high-end, unique, something the consumer couldn't get in any corner coffeehouse in Seattle. Haven't you noticed that the more exclusive something is, the more it's wanted?"

"You have a point there." She sipped on her ice water.

"But there is room for change, which is one of the reasons I wanted to bring you to lunch, among other things."

"Go on."

"I'd like Lillian's of Seattle to carry Myers Coffee Roasters. Both of our brands have a reputation for being the finest around, so I think it's a natural combination. What could be better than coffee with cake? What do you think?"

"Think? I think it's an excellent idea!" Mariah grinned unabashedly.

Everett was thrilled to hear the excitement in her voice at his pitch. He'd been thinking about it ever since he'd heard Lillian's was coming to Seattle. He'd never been a fan of Sweetness Bakery even though they had approached him about offering his coffee in their locations. Everett hadn't been interested in partnering with a bakery until now. Until Mariah.

"That's great!" He smiled broadly. "I was hoping you'd see that a partnership between us would be a good idea." And he wasn't talking just about business. Everett had known from the moment he'd seen Mariah that they would have more than a business relationship. There would be a personal one, too.

"I'll have to talk this over with my brothers first,"

Mariah replied. "But I don't see Chase or Jack vetoing an obviously great idea."

"Excellent! Then let's put business on the back burner and enjoy our lunch, which is just coming out now." The waitress returned with the salads.

When he dropped Mariah off less than an hour later, Everett couldn't resist watching her backside after he opened the bakery door for her. She was one fine looking woman and he was finally making headway. He just hoped that in time she would let down her guard so he could take their relationship to the next level. His gut told him that Mariah Drayson was a woman worth knowing, in every sense of the word.

Chapter 5

"Everett Myers wants to go into business with us?" Chase sat back on the couch in the bakery's office and absorbed the information that Mariah had just laid on him and Jackson after the store closed later that evening. She had been eager to spill the beans when she'd returned from lunch with Everett, but she'd kept Jackson in suspense throughout the day until she could fill them both in at the same time.

"Yep." Mariah beamed from ear to ear.

"I just knew that your good looks would come in handy one day." Jackson patted her back from the couch beside her.

"Jack!" She punched him in the shoulder.

"What?" He laughed. "You've got that man by the—" He'd been about to use a less than flattering word, but the look his older brother gave him halted him. "That man is falling for you so hard that he's willing to do anything to spend time with you, and that only works in our favor. We have to capitalize on it."

"I agree with Jack that the timing is great," Chase said more delicately. "Everett's offer gives us even more endorsement as the best bakery in town because his brand is high-end, with a solid reputation."

"We have to take it a step further," Jackson said, rising to his feet and pacing the floor. "We shouldn't just sell Myers Coffee Roasters, we should serve the java in the store."

"That's brilliant!" Chase jumped to his feet.

"Our initial concept included a café," Jackson continued. "With Myers's help, we can create a small café in the corner of the shop and serve coffee along with Lillian's pastries."

"And with a smart advertising campaign, we'd get all of the Myers coffee patrons coming into the bakery and build up our customer base," Chase added. "That's where you come in, sis." He pointed to her. "This is right up your alley."

"I'm getting excited, guys." Jackson rubbed his hands together in glee.

"So am I," Mariah said. "This could be the boost we need to set us apart from Sweetness Bakery."

"We'll bury them," Jackson stated. "And Everett Myers will get to spend more time with you in the process. It's a win-win for everybody."

Mariah snorted. "You just couldn't resist that dig, could ya, Jack?"

"Me?" He patted his chest as if he were innocent.

"Yes, you."

"C'mon, don't be mad." He pulled her to her feet, "Because before long we'll be in the black and success will be sweet."

"Yes, it will be."

Mariah was so excited at the prospect that she decided to call Everett and tell him the good news. He'd given her his business card with his private number already written on the back. It was as if he'd been waiting for just the right time to give it to her, even though she hadn't been compelled to give him hers. "Call me anytime," he'd said when he'd dropped her off after lunch, so she was going to do just that.

It was nearly 9:00 p.m. when she got to her apartment for the call. She hoped it wasn't too late, but she certainly wasn't about to phone him in front of her brothers. Jackson was already teasing her relentlessly about Everett's interest in her and she'd never live it down. She wanted to speak with him in the privacy of her own home.

"Hello?" His voice, when he answered, sounded breathless and in Mariah's opinion oh so sexy.

"Uh, hi. It's—it's Mariah," she said, stumbling over her words. "I hope I didn't catch you at a bad time?"

"No, you didn't. I was in the other room and heard the phone ringing. I have to say, though, I'm surprised to hear from you at this hour."

Mariah was surprised to be calling him, too. She could have easily waited until tomorrow and phoned him at the office, but for some reason she'd wanted to hear his voice before she went to bed. Perhaps so she could have another one of those erotic dreams she'd had since she'd met the man?

"Well, I was calling to tell you the good news. My brothers agreed that they'd like to go into business with you."

"That's great news, Mariah. I'm glad to hear it, though this could have waited until tomorrow."

"Are you upset that I called?" Her voice was shakier than she would have liked as she fell backward on her bed and nearly started hyperventilating. Had she miscalculated? Did he have someone else there with him? Was that why it was too late to call?

"Of course not," Everett answered smoothly. "I'm glad you did because it gives me hope."

"Hope for what?"

"That you might be as into me as I'm into you."

Mariah was quiet. Everett had a way of doing that to her, of being so blunt that she couldn't think of a pithy comeback. "Well, uh, we should get together tomorrow at the bakery perhaps and go over the details."

"I'm tied up during the day. How about dinner at 7:00 p.m. on Friday evening?"

If she looked up the word *relentless* in the dictionary, she would find a picture of Everett Myers. "I…" She wanted to turn him down, but didn't want to appear ungrateful for the incredible opportunity that had just landed in their lap, or jeopardize a potential business deal. And he damn well knew it. She had no choice but to capitulate. "Dinner is fine."

"Where shall I pick you up?"

Of course he wanted to pick her up, because in his mind this was a date, not a business dinner. She rattled off her address.

"I can't wait to see you, Mariah.," And just as she was hanging up she heard him whisper, "Dream of me."

Mariah hit the end button. Dream of him? Hell, she probably wouldn't be able to get him or the sound of his husky voice out of her mind. Tonight was one of those moments when she wished she kept a stress reducer in her nightstand drawer. Perhaps then she could relieve the ache between her thighs.

Everett smiled from the other end of the line after he'd hung up with Mariah, and lay back on the pillows of his king-size bed. He'd finally worn her down. She was finally starting to think of him outside of work. In her bed, perhaps? Was that where she was right now? He wondered what she was wearing. Was it one of those skimpy things women often wore to bed these days that they called pajamas? And was she thinking about him and what he would like to do to her? Did she know how much he would love to find out what secrets lay beneath the form-fitting clothes she wore? How much he wanted to taste her, and not just her mouth.

Everett took a deep breath to steady himself. He needed to get a grip because it would be a while before he unearthed all Mariah's secrets. But the best things in life were worth waiting for. He knew that the moment he had one taste of her, it would never be enough.

On Friday night, Everett excitedly rubbed his hands in eager anticipation of the romantic evening he had planned. Mariah had no idea what he had in store for her when he showed up at her apartment.

He was leaning in the entryway when she opened the door with a swish, and Everett nearly lost his footing. Mariah was spellbinding. She wore a beautiful concoction of a dress that was strapless and showed the swell of her breasts before swirling down to reveal the sway of her curvy hips.

He righted himself. "Good evening."

"So formal," Mariah said, closing the door behind her. She must have realized how rude she was because she said, "Forgive me. I guess I should have invited you in?"

Everett shook his head. "I only want an invitation when it's freely given and you want me there." When she invited him into her apartment, it was his hope that it would be an invitation to her bed and not just her space.

Mariah flushed visibly.

Everett shifted his arm and produced a bouquet of red roses he'd been holding behind his back. "For the lady."

She recovered and gave him a weak smile. "You shouldn't have, but thank you." She stepped away long enough to put the bouquet in a vase before returning to the foyer.

He offered her his arm. "Ready to go?"

Mariah was shocked when they got to the curb and found a stretch limousine waiting for them. She turned to Everett. "A limo?"

"I wanted to be able to drink and enjoy your company this evening. This was my compromise."

She nodded and accepted the hand he lent to help her. The inside was plush, with leather seats, a flat-screen television and a wet bar. Mariah supposed this was how the wealthy lived, but the only time she'd been in a limo had been to go to her high school prom.

Once Everett joined her, the limo seemed smaller inside. He filled up the entire space with his strong masculinity. He looked especially fine tonight in the black suit jacket and white silk shirt he wore. The matching trousers encasing his hard muscular thighs caused a shiver of awareness to course through Mariah. Her breasts tingled and she could feel her nipples pucker, tight and sensitive in the clingy fabric of her dress.

She watched as Everett leaned over the wet bar, producing a bottle of champagne, and two flutes that he handed to her. He popped the cork effortlessly and poured them each a glass. Afterward, he placed the bottle back in the ice bucket.

He seemed very comfortable in this environment and easily lifted his glass to say, "A toast."

"To the start of a great business relationship."

She suspected he'd wanted to say something else, but deferred to her and said, "Cheers."

She clinked her flute against his and took a sip of the champagne. It was fragrant and delicious. She couldn't resist a small moan.

"You like?"

She shook her head. "This is a great vintage."

"This is a celebration, right? So nothing but the best." He held her captive with the intensity of his gaze. Mariah had no choice but to stare back into his piercing dark eyes.

"Yes, it is." She saw his eyes roam over her face, lingering at her lips and she knew he wanted to kiss her, but he didn't. He reined in his passion and took another sip of his champagne. Mariah couldn't help but be a little disappointed, because if he'd gone for it, she wouldn't have stopped him.

"Were your brothers surprised by my offer to carry Myers coffee at the bakery?"

Mariah shook her head. "No. In fact, they took it a step further."

"How so?"

"Well…" She paused for effect. "We'd like to not only sell Myers Coffee Roasters, but have a café on-site so customers can purchase a hot cup of coffee, too. What do you think?"

His full lips curved into a genuine smile. "I think that's a wonderful idea," Everett said, "But I'd have to be involved in every stage of the planning if there's going to be a Myers Coffee Roasters café inside the bakery, albeit on a smaller scale."

"Of course," Mariah responded. "I wouldn't expect anything less. It is your brand, after all."

"You know what this means, right?"

She suspected she knew what he was angling for, but played dumb. "No, what does it mean?"

"It means, as part owner of Lillian's of Seattle, you and I will see an awful lot of each other as we get this venture off the ground. How do you feel about that?"

"I'm excited," she said, and watched as his eyes grew large. "For the bakery," she added, and noticed his smile lessen. "This is a huge coup for us."

He frowned. "Is that all that you see?"

She could tell that he wasn't happy with her response, and didn't know how to dig herself out of putting her foot in her mouth.

When she remained silent, he said, "Just so we're clear, the only Drayson I'm interested in working with is you. So if this project is going to be successful, I need to know you're on board with that. Are you?"

Chapter 6

Everett stared back at Mariah. He hoped his meaning was clear—that he wasn't backing down from trying to win her over and he would use any means necessary to spend time with her. A condition of this arrangement would be that he would work with Mariah and only Mariah.

She seemed to be mulling over his words for several long, agonizing moments, making Everett wonder if he'd pushed her too far, until she said, "Yes, I'm on board with that."

She didn't see his inward sigh of relief because outwardly he was all cool. He had to be for this to work. "Good." The limo came to a stop. "Looks like we're here."

Everett exited first and helped Mariah out. She was pleasantly surprised to see they were in front of the Space Needle.

"I thought we'd dine someplace special. C'mon." He took her hand and led her toward the entrance.

After they'd passed through the store and made their way to the elevators, Everett could see that Mariah was looking around and wondering where they were going. She probably thought they were dining at the SkyCity restaurant with its 360 degree panoramic view of Seattle. And he could have done that, but it would be expected. Instead, he'd rented a private room on the SkyLine level, where they could have dinner in private while being waited on hand and foot.

He intended to show Mariah that he could be thoughtful and romantic. Maybe then she'd see just how enamored he was with her. Hell, just being in the limo had been divine. Her warmth had surrounded him, enveloped him, and he'd wanted more.

When she'd moaned after tasting the champagne, his reaction had been instant and visceral. He wanted to take her in his arms and kiss her delectable mouth until she made the same pleasurable sounds with him, underneath him and because of him.

The attendant on the elevator stated, "You're here, Mr. Myers. Enjoy your evening."

The door swished open and they stepped out. Mariah looked at him questioningly. "Follow me," he said leading her to the Puget Sound room, where a maître d' was waiting for them.

"Good evening, sir," the man said. "Everything is set up as you desired."

Everett offered him his hand and slid him a hundred dollar tip. "Thank you."

The maître d' opened the double doors. "No, thank you. Enjoy."

The room was decorated just as he'd requested. Soft, muted lighting and candles were everywhere, along with a table for two in the center and a grand piano in the corner for later, when he intended to dance the night away in her arms.

He turned to Mariah. "What do you think?"

Mariah was awestruck at the effort Everett had gone through to arrange a private room for them, complete with a piano!

"Everett, this—this is amazing," she commented as she walked toward the windows. She could see the Olympic Mountains, downtown Seattle and the marina from here. No one had ever done anything like this for her, certainly not Richard. They'd been young and poor when they'd first started dating, and even later, after they'd graduated and started their respective careers, he couldn't have afforded to do anything this lavish. But Everett could and he had. She was truly touched.

She spun around to face him. "You didn't have to do all this."

He smiled at her. "I know that, but I *wanted* to. Now c'mon, sit. The chef has prepared a delicious meal for us."

While they ate their starters of crab claws and second course of baby spinach salad, and shared a bottle of wine, Mariah learned more about Everett and his family.

"So you're an only child?" she asked. "You're missing out." She smiled. "Chase, Jack and I have always been thick as thieves for as long as I can remember. You can imagine that, being the only girl, there were times I've had to tell them to back down if someone was giving me a hard time. You know how it is."

Everett laughed. "I can imagine how protective they must have been over you, their little sister. And your parents—how's your relationship with them?"

Mariah reached for her glass of wine. "For the most part, it's good."

He picked up on what she wasn't saying. "But not lately?"

She nodded. "They weren't happy that my brothers and I decided to go into the bakery business. They think it's beneath us. They'd much prefer if we stuck in our respective corners or joined Dad's real estate business. Chase is an accountant, Jack is an entrepreneur and in my previous life I was an advertising executive."

Everett quirked a brow. "Advertising? What happened? Why'd you leave?"

"It wasn't the right fit." Mariah was evasive, because she didn't really want to expound more on the topic. It could lead to other questions, such as the breakup of her marriage, but she knew she couldn't avoid the topic entirely this evening.

"I can understand," Everett replied. "Sometimes it takes time to find the right path."

"My blog certainly helped with showing me the way."

"You have a blog?"

She nodded. "It's called A Sista Who Bakes. I kinda used my Chicago cousins' idea of their Brothers Who Bake blog to form my own. I started it when baking was just a hobby, especially after my divorce."

"Why did you divorce? If you don't mind my asking." Everett dipped a claw into the warm butter sauce. Mariah watched him suck the succulent sweet meat from the shell and felt her inner muscles tighten in response.

She took a sip of her wine. She'd known when she'd agreed to this date that eventually they'd have to talk about their past relationships. "We got married young, right out of college, and over time…" she paused "…we drifted apart. So the blog was more cathartic than anything. You know, a way to escape."

"I can understand. Sara and I were both young when

we met, but we'd known each other for years before our relationship became romantic."

"Sounds wise." Mariah reached for a crab claw at the same time as Everett and the electricity just from that close encounter caused a lurch of excitement to surge through her. The very air around them was electrified and seemed to hum.

She tried to disengage it with her next comment. "So when Aunt Lillian mentioned opening another bakery in Seattle, after my divorce, the pieces fit into place. And it offered me a change of scene from Chicago."

"Your aunt is a pretty amazing woman," Everett commented. "I read about how she started the first bakery in the early sixties. It couldn't have been easy in Chicago."

"No, it wasn't. I guess it's why I admire her so much," Mariah said. "And want to make her proud."

"You will."

Mariah stared at Everett. He said it with such conviction that even she believed it. "I will with your help. Having a Myers Coffee Roasters café at the bakery, even on a small scale, is a huge bonus."

"Aw, it's not all that."

"Of course it is. Starbucks isn't the only game in town and you've got quite the following. And if I'm honest, I prefer yours."

"Really?"

"Don't sound so surprised. It has the right balance of flavor."

"It's what I was going for."

Everett continued to expound on how he got started in the coffee importing business when their entrées arrived. She'd ordered the herb-crusted halibut, while he'd opted for the wild king salmon.

Mariah sighed in contentment. "You weren't lying when

you said the chef had prepared a mouth-watering dinner for us. This is scrumptious." She took another forkful of halibut.

"I'm glad you're enjoying it."

"I'm not just enjoying the food," Mariah admitted. "I'm enjoying your company." She hadn't thought it was possible to feel this way again after Rich. Their breakup had been devastating to her self-esteem as a woman. Everett, however, was quickly boosting it in a big way.

He grinned, showing a flash of white teeth. "So am I."

Mariah's heart swelled in her chest. He didn't need to touch her to have her completely mesmerized. All he had to do was pin her with his razor-sharp gaze and she melted. She could easily be putty in his hands if she wasn't careful with her heart.

Everett stared at Mariah. He'd been watching her all night and he couldn't get enough of her. They'd just finished a decadent dessert of bananas Foster, which they'd both devoured. Mariah ate with passionate relish. She wasn't one of those women who picked at her meal. She wasn't afraid to be completely herself. There weren't any airs about her. What you saw was what you got. And it was refreshing.

He gave the maître d' a nod that it was time for the pianist to come in. "How about a dance?" Everett said, rising to his feet.

"There's no music."

"I'm sure we could make our own," he replied. At Mariah's surprised look, he inclined his head toward the man who was sitting down at the piano.

"I would love to." She rose to her feet just as the pianist began singing Nat King Cole's "Unforgettable."

The lights from the city and candlelight illuminated the

room, bathing Mariah in a soft glow. Everett held out his hand for her to join him on the dance floor.

He felt as if he'd waited a lifetime to finally have a legitimate reason to touch Mariah. He slid his arm around her slender waist, bringing her soft body into contact with his hard one. To her credit, Mariah tried to keep a respectable distance between the two of them, but Everett was having none of it. He wanted to *feel* her and he wasn't going to let her hesitancy get in the way.

At first, she was a little stiff when his other hand grasped hers, but eventually she gave in and moved her body closer to his. He dipped his head and placed it against the side of her face. Not only could he smell the fragrant sweetness of her perfume teasing his nostrils, but he could feel the heat emanating from her.

And from him. He was scorching hot for her. He could feel the rising bulge in his pants and couldn't resist crushing her body firmly to his. He thought Mariah would push him away as she felt the evidence of his arousal, but she didn't. He heard her breathing hitch and become labored. Was she feeling as turned on as he was?

Without thinking, he leaned forward and kissed her forehead. Then he lowered his head so he could trail hot kisses down the side of her face as he inched closer to her lips. He hadn't meant to do it and thought she might pull away, but she didn't. Instead, she looked up at him through sooty, mascara-covered lashes and he had the answer to his question. Desire gleamed in her eyes, just as he knew it did in his.

He bent down and brushed his lips softly over hers.

Mariah had known Everett was going to kiss her when she'd looked at him. His pupils had dilated and he'd stepped even closer to her, allowing her to feel the hard, unyielding pressure of his arousal against her middle. She was power-less to resist the pull, and her arms involuntarily moved up and over Everett's shoulders as he laid hungry siege to her lips. When he deepened the kiss, raking his tongue across her bottom lip, her lips parted of their own volition. The touch of his tongue on hers sent a jolt of electricity spark-ing inside her. Her entire body awakened at the contact and she knew that he wanted her.

Right here.

Right now.

His hands moved caressingly down the length of her spine and rested on her hips. She suspected he was going to cup her bottom, but given that they had an audience, thought better of it. That's what jolted her out of the kiss, and she wrenched her mouth from his. She tried unsuc-cessfully to pull out of his arms. His hold on her was too tight. "Everett…"

"Hmm…?"

"There are people here," she whispered into his ear.

"I'm aware of that. Why else do you think I haven't ravished you on the spot?"

She glanced up at him and saw the devilry in his eyes. He was teasing her. "Perhaps we should…"

"Stop?" he asked, his gaze hooded. "That's a negative. If I promise to be good, will you let me hold you?"

The sexual potency Everett had just wreaked on her body told Mariah it wasn't a good idea, but it felt so good to be in a man's arms again. And not just any man's, but Everett's. She couldn't say no even if she tried to. "Okay."

They continued dancing to several songs, until Everett took a step backward. "Thank you."

She nodded. Had he known what that had cost her? To not retreat and run at the first sign that their relationship had taken a sudden shift in direction?

"How about we go to the observation deck to finish off the evening?" Everett offered.

"I'd like that."

Several minutes later, they were looking out over the city of Seattle, standing hand in hand. They were both silent as they took in the lights and the stars overhead. Mariah could still feel the current of sizzling chemistry passing back and forth between them. It was so palpable that her heart was hammering in her chest. Was it taking as much restraint on Everett's part as it was on hers for them not to kiss again?

But he kept his word and didn't kiss her. Instead, after a short time on the observation deck, he took her to the limo and they drove back to her apartment.

Mariah appreciated that Everett was respecting her wishes and doing the honorable thing, but had to admit she wouldn't have minded if he'd been a bit of a bad boy and stolen another kiss.

When they reached her place, he kept the limo idling as he walked her inside and up the stairs to her second-floor apartment. "Thank you for a lovely evening," she said in her doorway.

"I aim to please," he said with a bow.

She laughed. He truly was a remarkable man, and maybe in another life things might be different, but she doubted there would ever be more than this moment. She couldn't let it. She couldn't afford to get close and let another man in, only to have it not work out after he realized she wasn't a whole woman.

"We'll talk soon about the café…" She left the sentence hanging and turned toward the door.

That's when Everett surprised her and reached for her once more. And this time they didn't have an audience. He backed her up against the door, cupped her bottom and pulled her firmly and snugly against the pulsing length of his rock-hard erection. Mariah gasped and Everett used her shock to insert his tongue deep inside her mouth. Then one of his hands came upward to cup her breasts over the softness of the chiffon material. He brushed his thumb over her nipple and it hardened on the spot. Everett groaned and shifted the hardness of his shaft even closer into her core.

Mariah knew her panties were damp with moisture as he fully explored every inch of her mouth before tangling her tongue with his. His tongue continued to stroke hers over and over with such achingly slow flicks that she thought she'd die on the spot from so much pleasure. She was no expert in the lovemaking department, but she reciprocated his movements and hoped he was enjoying the kiss as much as she.

When he lifted his head, his eyes were dark with desire. "I wish I could say I was sorry about that, but I just had to have another taste of you. I'll see you tomorrow."

Seconds later, he was gone, leaving Mariah breathing hard and desperate for more.

Everett wasn't sure how he made it back to the limousine, given the painfully hard erection he was now sporting. If he hadn't left, he would have taken the keys from Mariah's hand and backed her up into her apartment, invitation or not. Then he would show her exactly how much he desired her, and vice versa.

He wasn't sure of much, but he was certain Mariah had wanted him to kiss her again. He'd felt her yearning, her craving to have his tongue in her mouth in the limo, and he'd had to oblige. Now all he had to do was figure out how he was going to pull back. Tonight, he'd shown Mariah his romantic and passionate side, but he also wanted her to see his restraint and that he could wait until she was ready to invite him into her bed.

During the evening, he'd sensed that she didn't have much experience in the dating department. Not that he'd had tons himself, but he'd sensed her nervousness even though she'd tried to mask it with conversation. Despite her nerves, she'd responded to him with abandoned enthusiasm, which made him even more of an admirer. He couldn't wait to see where their relationship would go next.

Chapter 7

"Well, look who the cat dragged in," Jackson said, when Mariah arrived late to the bakery on Saturday morning.

"Not today, Jack," Mariah cautioned. She'd slept fitfully the night before, all because of one man. Everett. How dare he get her so turned on and then just leave? Not that she'd ever be one for casual sex—heck, her ex-husband was her first and only lover—but she certainly didn't like being left high and dry!

Last night, Everett had kissed her senseless and turned on every dormant hormone in her body, so much so that she'd dreamed of him and awoke with an ache between her legs that only one thing could satisfy.

"What's got you in a huff?" Jackson asked.

"Nothing!" She grabbed her apron and tied it around her neck and waist, then began clanging pots and bowls as she prepared her station.

"Doesn't look like nothing to me," her brother responded. "It's not like you to be late or ill-tempered. That's my department."

"Well, you don't have the lock on being a jerk," she said, finally offering him a smile.

"Ah, now there's the Mariah I know." He continued kneading the dough he was working on. "I'd think you'd be on cloud nine since you convinced your admirer to invest in our bakery."

Mariah thought about Everett and then her mind wandered to his lips and how his bottom lip was fuller than the top. She remembered how she'd sucked on it last night with fervor. "I am happy."

"Coulda fooled me. What did lover boy say about our café idea? Was he on board?"

Mariah nodded. "He loved it, but insisted that he would be heavily involved with the concept from start to finish."

"Sounds reasonable. His name is on it."

She turned her back to grab some flour out of the pantry and added, "He wants to work exclusively with me on the project."

She didn't hear Jackson sneak up on her until he spun her around. "Are you sure you're not in over your head on this?"

Mariah pulled away from her brother. "Of course not. I can handle this expansion and Everett."

Jackson held up his hands. "All right, as long as you're sure, because Myers isn't interested in just the café."

Mariah tried grabbing the large bag of flour, but Jack took it out of her hands and carried it over to her station.

"Thank you, and I'm aware of Everett's intentions."

"It's Everett now?" Surprise laced her brother's voice.

"Yes. We went to dinner last night and—"

Jackson held up his hands. "Wait a second, you and

Myers went to dinner and you didn't lead with that? Is that what has you in a mood today? Did something happen last night? Did he do something untoward? If so, I can go over to his office and knock his block off."

Mariah suppressed a soft gurgle of laughter. "As much as I appreciate this brotherly affection, it's not necessary. I'm capable of taking care of myself. Furthermore, nothing happened that I didn't want to happen."

Jackson's eyes grew large like saucers. "So, something did happen?"

"I don't intend on discussing my love life with my brother, so drop it, okay?"

"Now he's part of your love life? Oh, Lord!" Jackson threw his hands up in the air again. "All I can say is be careful, since I don't want anything to get in the way of this project. It's too important for Lillian's."

"And it won't. I've got it covered."

"All right."

It sounded to Mariah as if Jackson didn't believe her, but she didn't care. She would deal with Everett in her own way. First by keeping their relationship on a more businesslike footing while the café was in process. Jackson was right about that. She couldn't afford for anything to jeopardize this opportunity, not even her interest in the man behind it.

Everett woke up with a smile on his face. He had finally sampled sweet Mariah and the taste had stayed with him all weekend. So much so that when he'd turned over he'd fully expected her to be lying beside him on the king-size bed. She hadn't been, but now Everett knew with certainty that he and Mariah would become lovers.

For days she'd tried to act as if she was unaffected by

him, but Friday night she'd given in to her own desires. And when he'd kissed her, she'd kissed him back. And it wasn't a demure kiss, but one full of fire and passion and a hunger like the one that had been building inside him from the moment they'd met.

When he'd cradled her in his arms in front of her apartment and his shaft had cocooned itself in her softness, he'd felt as if he was home. It had taken every bit of self-restraint for him to refrain from acting on his deepest desires, but he had to. Despite how responsive she was, Everett knew he had to tread lightly. If he came on too strong again, she'd retreat, and he didn't want that. It's why he'd decided not to visit today, but give her time to absorb everything that had happened between them.

Keeping his distance while working with Mariah on the Myers Coffee Roasters café was going to be extremely difficult, but he had to. He would visit the bakery every day as he'd done before, or whenever he could. He wanted Mariah to become comfortable with having him as a part of her life, so the transition from business partners to lovers would feel seamless.

"Penny for your thoughts?" His mother was standing in the doorway of his office on Monday morning.

"Mom, this is a pleasant surprise," Everett said, rising to his feet. "What are you doing here?"

"I was in the neighborhood for a charity meeting and figured I'd stop by and check in on you. How are you? And how's my darling grandbaby?"

Everett glanced at his mother. Gwen Myers was still stunning at fifty-eight. Her smooth café-au-lait skin showed no signs of aging and was expertly made up to go along with the Dior suit she wore with matching pumps.

"I'm doing great and EJ, well, he's had a bit of a tough

week at school, and especially at this time of year. But he'll pull through."

She sat down on the sofa along one wall. "What's going on?"

Everett sat beside her and filled her in on the bullying at school and EJ's response to not having a mother.

Gwen touched her chest in horror. "Oh, that poor baby. Everett, what can I do?"

"I'm sure a visit from Grandma would help tremendously and give him a bit of the mother figure he so desperately craves. Other than that, I'm not sure what else would help."

"I so wished you would have remarried after Sara." When she saw the stricken look on his face, his mother quickly added, "More so for EJ than for you, my boy." She patted his thigh. "Then he would have a mom."

"He has one."

"You know what I meant."

"I'm sorry, Mom." Everett rose from the couch, walked over to the window and stared at Elliott Bay. "I've always wondered that myself. Did I do him a disservice by shunning all those women? But the thing is—" he turned to face her "—I never really felt like any of them were genuine, but now…" His voice trailed off as he thought of Mariah Drayson.

His mother was perceptive and asked, "And now what?"

"Excuse me?" He turned around.

"I asked now what, but you looked a million miles away. Like you were thinking of something, or should I say some*one*?"

Everett tried to smother a smile, but his mother rose from the sofa and reached for both his hands. "Have you met someone?"

He nodded.

"You have?" Her voice rose slightly. "Oh, Everett, I'm so happy for you. Who is she? When can I meet her? What does EJ think of her?"

"Mom, slow down," Everett said, releasing her hands. "We haven't gotten that far yet. We only just met, but there's something about her that's different from the women I've met since Sara. She's special."

"Don't leave me in suspense. What's her name?"

"Her name is Mariah Drayson."

"Of the Seattle Draysons?" his mother inquired. "I've heard of them. Nadia Drayson sits on one of my charities and she's having a ball at the Myers Hotel later this summer, while your father has had some real estate business dealings with Graham Drayson."

"Yes, the same Draysons," Everett responded. "Mariah recently opened a bakery called Lillian's of Seattle."

His mother obviously didn't recognize the name, just stared at him blankly. "Lillian's is a popular bakery on Chicago's Magnificent Mile and they won a television competition a few years ago."

"That's excellent, darling. At least she comes from a family of good standing. Having a store on the Magnificent Mile is very exclusive."

"Mom, you realize you sound very snobby."

She looked chagrined. "I only want the best for my son."

Everett wrapped his arm around her shoulders and pulled her toward him in a hug. "I know, and I love you, too. But if I truly liked her, I wouldn't care where she came from, only how good her heart is."

"You can't be so naive, darling. You have to think about EJ with whoever you date, and whether she would be a good mother."

"EJ is never far from my mind," he said, even though he had to admit he hadn't been thinking of his son last night when he'd had Mariah backed up against the door of her apartment. "I will always put his interests and well-being above my own."

"Oh, I know you will. And you think this woman, this Mariah, could be a possibility?"

"It's too early to say, but something tells me the answer is yes."

Just before closing time on Monday, Mariah wiped down the counters. It had been a rather slow day and not seeing Everett all weekend or today had only added to her disappointment. She knew it was silly, but she'd started to look forward to his daily visits, count on them. She knew it was wrong, especially when she intended to halt any ideas of a blossoming romance that might get into his head after her scandalous behavior Friday night.

She'd had no intention of getting *that* close to him. All she could do was chalk it up to the romance of the evening. Everett had pulled out all the stops with the private dinner at the Space Needle, the champagne and the pianist. What woman wouldn't get caught up in the moment? It didn't help that he was nerve-sizzlingly attractive and that whenever he was around, her brain short-circuited and she lost herself.

His kisses had rocked her to her core, making her weak at the knees and fisting handfuls of his suit jacket in an effort to keep from falling. The strong chin, chiseled cheekbones, sexy dark eyes and irresistible smile combined with a hard, muscled and toned body had made Mariah want to throw propriety to the wind and ask him inside her apartment. If she'd done that, she was sure that Everett would have given her one helluva mind-blowing climax. He'd almost made her orgasm just from a kiss.

If she was honest, Richard had never made her feel that

way. They'd been young kids in love and figuring out each other's bodies. And yes, they'd grown together, eventually discovering what pleased each other. But none of their experiences had come close to what Everett had made her feel from his kisses and caresses. She could only imagine that she would probably faint from the passion and intensity of Everett full throttle. As intense as he was, she was glad he'd had the common sense to end things Friday night.

Had he regretted his actions? Was that why he hadn't visited the bakery since? Or were her kisses so abhorrent that it made him want to run in the opposite direction? She didn't have much to compare him to, but she'd given him as much of herself as she was capable of under the circumstances.

She wished she had someone to confide in. Most of her friends back in Chicago were married couples, and she didn't think they would understand what it was like to be newly single. She hadn't been back in Seattle long enough to make any new friends, and most of her crowd from high school had dispersed to other parts of the country.

And as far as her family went, she most certainly couldn't talk to her brothers about her love life, even though Jack always wanted to be in her business. Her mother had never been much into girl talk. But there was always Belinda in Chicago.

Mariah shook her head. Why was she second-guessing herself, anyway? Hadn't she said that she and Everett should keep things professional? The next time she saw him, she would act as if the date hadn't happened.

Just as she was about to close the bakery for the day, Everett showed up with preliminary sketches from his interior designer, along with the name of the general contractor he wanted to use to carve out the café space.

"Wait, wait," Mariah said. "Take a breath."

He'd walked in full of fire and zest for the project and sat down at a table with the sketches. There hadn't been his usual hello and flirtatious greeting; he'd gotten right down to business. Had he forgotten her kisses that quickly?

She surely hadn't, and it didn't help that he looked handsome as usual. He was wearing trousers and a button-down shirt instead of his usual suit.

He grinned abashedly. "I'm sorry—I'm so excited about the project that I couldn't resist taking the first step and coming up with a layout. I hope you don't mind?"

Mariah shook her head. "Of course not. You know more about the coffee business and what would be required." She looked over the drawings. "How did you get a copy of our layout?"

He shrugged. "Your permit is part of the public record and I have a few friends in the department."

Mariah bristled. It must be nice to have friends in high places. "It would also have been nice if you'd asked."

"Of course, I'm sorry. I'm sure you'd like to look this over with your brothers and get back to me. As I told you, I want to be involved in all facets of this project."

She couldn't forget. "And you still want me to run lead?"

He stared at her piercingly. "Yes, I still want you."

Mariah swallowed audibly. There it was again—that innuendo in his words. Add the way he was looking at her, as if she was the cherry on top of a hot fudge sundae, and it told her that perhaps he wasn't all about business, either, and that there was still a part of him that desired her. If she was honest, it soothed her female ego after his no-show all weekend and his right-to-business tactics now. "That's good to hear."

His full lips curved into a smile. "Great, because I'd like to bring some contractors by tomorrow so we can start getting this priced out."

"You sure don't waste any time, do you?"

"Why should I? I'm certain you're as eager as I am to get this project off the ground, especially for a start-up business."

"Well, yes, but we're not in dire straits. We've only been open a week." Mariah bristled again. She didn't appreciate Everett acting as if they were a lost cause and he was doing them a favor. Lillian's of Seattle would make it with him or without him. She would see to it, because she wouldn't let it fail.

Heck, just this morning she'd been working on a new creation. She wasn't sure of the name yet, but once she'd perfected it, Mariah just knew it would sell like hotcakes.

"I'm sorry," Everett said. "I didn't mean to insinuate otherwise. I'm here to help."

"Of course, and I'm sorry if I'm a little sensitive on the topic." She offered him a weak smile.

"Did something happen?" he inquired.

"No, not exactly, but my brothers and I have been summoned home for a family powwow dinner tonight. I'm sure it'll be just another attempt by our parents to convince us we made a poor decision by opening the bakery."

"Don't let their negativity get you down," Everett said. "Use it to fuel your passion and your determination to succeed. Show them *they* made the mistake by not supporting your dreams."

Mariah stared at him incredulously. She couldn't believe how impassioned his speech was, and he barely knew her.

"Don't look so surprised. I didn't get where I am without ambition and the drive to succeed."

"No, I don't suppose you did." And she'd had it herself once, before her marriage had gone to hell in a handbasket.

"So, it's all right if I bring some contractors by in the morning?"

Mariah nodded. "Absolutely. I'm sure this layout will work just fine, but I'll run it past my brothers."

Everett rose to his feet, towering over her. "You do that. In the meantime, I have to get going." He reached for his briefcase and started toward the door.

"Oh, okay." Mariah hated to admit she was enjoying his company and didn't want to see him go.

He must have heard something in her voice, because he said, "How about a kiss for the road?"

Chapter 8

"Baby girl." Her father planted a kiss on her cheek as Mariah entered the foyer of her childhood home later that evening. Although Everett hadn't gotten the kiss for the road, she had been happy to see him, and now it was family time.

"It's good to see you, Daddy." Mariah gave him a quick squeeze around his shoulders. She'd always been a daddy's girl and treasured the special bond that existed between the two of them. "You're looking well."

Even at fifty-nine, her father was a handsome man with his smooth, honey-toned skin. From his dark, close-cropped hair to his bushy eyebrows and ever present mustache, Graham Drayson was debonair. He was a suit-and-tie kind of guy, but tonight he wore trousers and a pullover sweater.

"C'mon, everyone's in the back."

"Including Mom?"

"Oh, don't be like that." He knew that at times Mariah's relationship with her mother was like oil and water.

But her father had loved her mother from the moment he'd met her, and it had been that way ever since. When Mariah had told him her marriage to Richard was over, he'd had a hard time understanding and accepting it. For her father, marriage was a life-long commitment. She respected that about him, along with the fact that he was a self-made man who'd done well for himself as a savvy real estate agent, consequently being able to give her and her brothers an upper-middle-class background.

Just look at what he'd done with their home. The stunning Queen Anne Victorian overlooked the water in one of Seattle's most exclusive neighborhoods. It had stained glass windows, a turret and sprawling landscaped grounds that her mother kept meticulously manicured. Nadia Drayson had initially hated the house, telling her father he was a fool for purchasing the ramshackle place, but Graham had seen the potential and called it "a diamond in the rough," then had lovingly restored it himself. It may have taken years, but her mother had finally come to adore the house, and it was her father's pride and joy.

"I'll try," Mariah finally said, as he led her by the arm into the family room, where Chase, Jackson and her mother were already seated around the large, sixty-inch flat-screen television. Her brothers were drinking beers, while her mom held a glass of red wine.

"Hey, sis." Jackson rose to greet her. "What's that you got there in your arms?"

Mariah glanced down. She'd forgotten that she'd brought the blueprints Everett had dropped off earlier, so she could get Chase and Jack's opinion. "These are the drawings I mentioned to you earlier."

Chase must have been eavesdropping because he said,

"Oh, yeah, let me see." He was jumping off the couch when her mother sidestepped him and came toward Mariah with her arms outstretched.

Mariah suffered through the obligatory kisses on either cheek. "Mom, how are you?"

Nadia pulled away and studied Mariah from head to toe. "I'm well, but I'm not sure I can say the same for you. What are you wearing? What's happened to you since you've been back in Seattle? When you were in Chicago you were always so elegantly dressed."

And here it goes, Mariah thought. The criticism, the put-downs. Could she ever do anything right in this woman's eyes?

Probably not. At fifty-seven years old, her mother was extremely polished and an impeccable dresser. She wouldn't be caught dead in Mariah's outfit of a simple shirt dress, which she'd belted at the waist and teamed with riding boots. Her mother had straight black hair and refused to allow herself to go gray, by monthly salon visits. Nadia Drayson lived the easy life, having long since stopped helping her husband build his real estate business, and shifting her focus to charity work instead.

"I'm sorry, Mom, but now that I'm a baker I don't see the point in wearing sheath dresses and Louboutin shoes."

Her mother gasped. "Oh, the horror. You can't speak ill of Louboutins."

Mariah couldn't suppress the gurgle of laughter that escaped her lips, and apparently neither could her brothers, who were standing nearby and probably waiting for World War III to erupt between them, which usually happened when they were within six feet of each other. But tonight was different. Mariah wasn't going to let her mother ruffle her feathers.

She held up the blueprints and glanced at her brothers.

"I thought we could look these over before dinner. That's if it's not ready yet?" She stared at her mother questioningly.

Nadia waved her hand, "Oh, that's fine, but don't take too long. I like my duck moist."

Mariah chuckled as she, Chase and Jackson walked down the hall to their father's study.

"So, let's see them," Chase said, pulling the prints from under her arm.

He unrolled the large drawings and spread them out over the table adjacent to her father's massive oak desk. She'd always loved that desk and sitting on his lap as she'd watch him work.

Chase studied the plans for several long minutes, going around the table to view them from all angles. "These are great."

"I know. That's what I thought" Mariah understood the basics about reading the drawings because she'd been involved in the bakery's design. Everett's designer had come up with an efficient use of the small space, while not taking away anything from the bakery.

"I agree," Jackson said, looking over her shoulder, "The plans even show some shop drawings of the displays that would house the Myers Coffee Roasters product. He thought of everything."

"He did say he wanted to be involved with every facet of the project," Mariah reminded them.

Chase looked up from the drawings and pushed his wire-rimmed glasses back into place on his nose. "How do you feel about that? I mean, you are the reason he's doing all this."

"Am not." Mariah knew it was a childish response as soon as she uttered it, but she couldn't help herself sometimes. Being around her older brothers made her revert to being a kid.

Jackson stared at her with those light brown eyes of his as if he couldn't believe she was actually lying to their faces.

"It may have been part of the reason," Mariah amended, "that Everett decided to partner with us, but it's good business. He wouldn't be doing this otherwise. I highly doubt he's doing this to lose money."

"Perhaps, but he could be doing it to get a piece of—"

Mariah pointed her finger at him. "Don't you dare, Jackson Drayson!" she warned.

Jackson flushed and had the decency to look embarrassed at what he'd been about to say to his younger sister. "Sorry, kid," He pulled her into the crook of his arm. "You know I wouldn't let some guy play you. I've got your back."

Mariah stared up at him. "I know." But she couldn't resist jabbing him in the ribs for the barb.

"Ouch!" Jackson feigned being hurt even though Mariah knew her punch had hit the brick wall that was his abdomen. Jackson believed in staying fit and toned. It was why the women flocked to him—his body and that good-looking face.

"So, now that we're all on board," Chase said, getting back down to business, "you'll let Everett know we approve, and get some pricing on this? We'll need three competitive bids, as we'll be responsible for half the costs."

"Why should we pay? When he came to us?" Jackson asked.

"Because we want a stake in the profit," Chase responded. "Mariah, do you want to discuss a percentage with Myers or shall I? I'll only ask for what's fair."

"No need. I already have a number in mind."

Chase stepped backward. "So, it's like that?"

Mariah smirked. "Don't underestimate me."

* * *

Mariah wished dinner could have gone as smoothly as her business conversation with her brothers had. They'd made it through salad and her mother's famous pretzel bread and were on the entrée course of orange duck when Nadia Drayson decided she wanted to revisit why her children had insisted on opening a bakery against her and their father's wishes.

Mariah suspected it was her mother's wishes and her dad had just gone along. As the old saying went, "happy wife, happy life." Mariah couldn't fault him for that, but wasn't about to listen to this same old love song again. What was done was done and their mom was just going to have to accept their decision.

"I don't understand why you did it," Nadia said. "Didn't we give you all the very best in life? The very best education? The world was your oyster. But instead you choose to open up a bakery and do manual labor?" She shook her head in despair. "I just don't understand."

"And you don't have to," Mariah snapped.

"Easy now," Graham admonished.

Mariah glanced up and saw her father's reproachful look. He didn't appreciate the way she'd spoken to her mother.

She forced herself to say, "I'm sorry, Mom, but you have to understand. This is a great opportunity for us to build something on our own. Aunt Lillian has given us the tools with her great recipes, and with some of our new ones, I know we'll do great."

"But it's a fickle business," her mother pressed. "Right now everyone is into health fads and gluten-free—it's poor timing. You should return to what you went to school for, advertising. It was your passion until...until—"

Everyone around the table stopped breathing at what they knew was coming.

"Until what?" Mariah asked through clenched teeth.

Her mother glanced up and faced her head-on. "Until your infertility. You were perfectly happy with your career and then you got obsessed with baby making at the exclusion of everything."

"So you're saying that the divorce was all *my* fault?"

"Nadia," her father interjected, "you need to—"

But her mother interrupted him. "Well, yes," she answered unapologetically before taking a sip of wine. "Haven't I always told you to put your man first, like I do your father?" She glanced across the table at her adoring husband. "Perhaps if you'd focused more on your marriage, you might still be together today."

Mariah was stunned by her mother's words. "Is that what you all think, too?" She glanced at Chase, who held his head down, and Jackson, who rolled his eyes upward, while her father looked appropriately chagrined.

When no one answered, she threw her napkin on her plate and rose to her feet. "Excuse me, I think I'll have my dinner elsewhere." She spun on her heel and fled from the room.

She heard the pleas of her father, "Wait! Mariah, wait!" Tears blinded her eyes. She just had to get out of there.

Once she made it to her car, Mariah let out a long, tortured sigh. She glanced up at the house. Her own family thought she'd been cuckoo for Cocoa Puffs by putting all her energy into trying to have a baby. They just didn't get why it was so important to her. The need and desire to have someone who would love her unconditionally was so strong, Mariah thought she would die when she'd learned she might not ever conceive. It seemed like a cruel twist of fate. But that was her lot in life and she was going to have to accept it, no matter how much it hurt.

Everett was exhausted and Friday hadn't come quick enough for him. He'd just gotten back from an unplanned trip to Vegas to check on one of the Myers Hotels. They'd had an unexpected hiccup with construction at the new location, so he'd had to leave EJ with his parents and fly there to straighten out the mess. He hadn't intended on staying three days, but he'd had to deal with some city officials to ensure the project got off the ground.

He was happy to be home in Seattle. EJ was so excited to see him last night that he'd stayed up well past his usual bedtime to be with him. Everett had been just as excited to see him and planned to spend some quality father-son time this weekend.

Everett also wasn't too happy with the fact that he'd gone three whole days without seeing the gorgeous honey blonde. Right when he was starting to make headway and Mariah was getting used to his visits, he'd had to leave unexpectedly. He just hoped he hadn't lost ground.

Which was why he was surprised when his receptionist informed him that Mariah Drayson had arrived and wished to see him. Everett sat up straight and straightened his silk tie. This was an unexpected surprise, but one that pleased him immensely. "Show her in."

Several moments later, Mariah strode into his office carrying what looked to be the blueprints he'd given her several days ago. "Good morning." She offered him a smile. "I hope I didn't catch you at a bad time."

He rose from his chair and walked toward her to greet her. "Not at all. It's good to see you, albeit a surprise."

She looked scrumptious in a suit with a laced up detail along the side of the jacket and pencil skirt, along with some sexy black pumps. He'd love to unlace every inch of that skirt so he could run his hands over the generous amount of leg she revealed. Had she worn this sexy outfit just for him? If so, he wholeheartedly approved.

Her hair was loosely curled around her face and her eyes were bright. "I'm sure. Usually it's you coming to me," she replied. "But I thought it appropriate that I come to you this time, since the offer and design you've presented to us is pretty irresistible."

"Pretty irresistible?" He flashed a grin. "Is that all? I was hoping for fantastic, magnificent and any other adjective you can think of."

Mariah laughed. "It's all of those things, with one caveat." She took a seat on the chair facing his desk.

"What's that?" he said, leaning his backside against the desk to face her.

"We want 40 percent."

"That's a large sum," Everett said, eyeing her warily. He shouldn't be surprised that she'd done her homework; Mariah struck him as a savvy businesswoman.

"Yes, but we're prepared to pay half the costs of the renovation."

"Considering you're a start-up in Seattle, I would think you'd need to keep your capital in reserve."

"True, but this investment is worth the risk."

"Well said, but I'm not giving you 40 percent."

She cocked a brow, obviously surprised at his firm tone. Perhaps she thought she could sweet-talk him into it? And perhaps she could; it would depend on what the lady was willing to give him in return.

"Would you settle for thirty?"

"Hmm…" He rubbed his chin thoughtfully. "How about twenty-five?"

She smiled. "You drive a hard bargain, but I'm sold.

We have a deal." She offered her hand for him to shake, but instead of doing so, he used it to pull her toward him into his arms.

Everett didn't know what came over him. He hadn't intended to act on his impulse, but he'd missed her. A week was too long and he just had to kiss her. He lowered his head and, to her stunned surprise, brushed his lips across hers. He moved deliberately and with expert precision, but slowly and gently until she softened and her body strained to be closer to him, while her lips became more pliant.

When she sighed, he dipped his tongue deep inside her mouth and tasted her with leisurely licks and flicks. He delved deeper, mating his tongue with hers, and she raised her arms to circle around his neck. He growled and cupped the back of her head so he could kiss her more thoroughly.

Eventually, he pulled away, leaving them both panting and breathless.

Mariah touched her lips. "Everett, w-what was that?"

"I was sealing our arrangement with a kiss."

"A handshake might have been more appropriate under the circumstances."

"But not nearly as much fun," he responded, his voice husky.

"I have to go." Mariah quickly exited the room, much to Everett's chagrin. He would have loved for her to stay and barter with him. Show him that she was just as affected as he was by that kiss, but she was still fighting the attraction between them. *That's okay*, he thought. Because in time she would see that it was inevitable for them to become more than business partners.

"C'mon, you can't still be mad at me," Jackson said later that morning when she finally made it to the bakery. She'd left a message for both her brothers that she'd had business the previous evening and both of them had better be present to open up in the morning.

Both Chase and Jackson had been stunned by her declaration and each had left her several text messages, but she hadn't responded. She was still furious with them for not standing up to their mother when she went on the attack on Monday night. Mariah had been giving them the silent treatment the last few days. They were supposed to speak up for her, protect her. Instead, they'd let their mother bully her, which was par for the course, but she'd expected more from them. Adding insult to injury was their failure to state they didn't think Mariah's infertility or single-minded obsession with getting pregnant was the cause of her divorce.

"Yeah, we're sorry." Chase came toward her as she walked into the kitchen and reached for her apron on the hook. "Really sorry. I should have stepped in and stopped Mom from bashing you, and I apologize that I didn't protect you, little sis."

Mariah glanced up with unshed tears in her eyes and nodded. Chase grasped her in his arms, picked her up and squeezed her in a bear hug.

"I love you, kid," he said. "Always have, ever since I saw you in the hospital and you came out of the womb bald as an eagle."

Mariah couldn't resist a laugh as he lowered her to the floor. "I was not bald."

"Was too," Jackson said, coming over to the duo. "Chase and I wondered if you were a boy because you didn't have any hair, and Dad really wanted a girl to dote on."

"And he got you," Chase said, caressing her cheek.

Mariah sniffed. It had been hard staying mad at her brothers for this long. It just wasn't part of her makeup.

She was the forgive-and-forget type. "So, how have you guys fared without me and Nancy?"

The older woman had been out all week with the flu, so even Chase had had to pitch in, roll up his dress shirt sleeves and help out. He might not know much about baking, but he could mix ingredients, roll out dough and cut it with a cookie cutter. Jackson and Mariah would do all the heavy lifting.

"Where were you, anyway?" Jackson inquired.

Mariah smiled inwardly. First she'd done something for herself and slept in until 7:00 a.m., if you could call that sleeping in. Something she never did. Was it to teach the boys a lesson? Sure, but she had enjoyed the extra hours of shut-eye.

By eight, she'd made her way toward Everett's office. Given his initial exuberance, she'd been surprised when he'd backed off and granted her some space, a week's time to be exact, to agree to a partnership between them. His risk had paid off. She'd come to him. She'd taken a chance that he was an early riser and he was. Was he surprised by her visit to his office? Yes, but he'd quickly recovered and stolen a kiss. When he'd drawn her toward him, it had been as if he was pulling her into some sort of force field. The sheer strength and demand of his will forced her to comply, to allow herself to be kissed thoroughly. That's when everything around them ceased to exist and she could think only of Everett and his searing kisses. Kisses that drove her mad until she'd had no choice but to run.

"Earth to Mariah!"

"What?" she asked, annoyed. She didn't appreciate having her daydream of Everett's full soft lips on hers interrupted.

"I asked where you were," Jackson replied. "No need to get snippy."

Mariah turned to face him. "I had a meeting with Everett and let him know our demands."

"And?" Chase stopped kneading the dough he'd returned to.

"He agreed to 25 percent," Mariah stated.

"He did?" Chase and Jackson asked in unison.

Mariah nodded excitedly. "Sure did. There was some discussion back and forth, but eventually he came around to my way of thinking."

Jackson's eyes narrowed. "And exactly what did you have to do to get him to see things your way?"

Mariah rolled her eyes at her older brother. "Get your mind out of the gutter, Jack. Anyway, what does it matter? His lawyer will draft up the agreement and this café will be up and running in no time!"

Chase walked back toward her and extended his hand, which Mariah shook. "I have to hand it to you, sis. I wasn't sure you could pull this off, but you did. You're right about one thing."

"Me?" She placed her hand on her chest. "Right about something?" She feigned scorn.

"Yeah, you were right that we underestimate you," Chase responded. "But I won't make that mistake again."

Mariah grinned unabashedly. Everett had learned the same thing today when he'd thought she would give in, but she'd stood her ground and walked away with a fair percentage for the business. She'd won personally, too, because he had made it clear with that kiss that he wasn't backing down from developing their relationship. And if she was honest with herself, she was looking forward to him trying.

Chapter 9

"A café inside the bakery?" Lillian Drayson asked over the phone when Mariah, Chase and Jackson shared the news with her and the entire Chicago Drayson clan in a conference call the following Monday morning.

"Yes," Chase replied. "In addition to selling Myers Coffee Roasters, a well-known brand in Seattle, they'll be setting up a café inside the bakery, selling cappuccinos, lattes and more."

There was applause in the background and Mariah looked at her brothers and beamed with pride.

"I think it's an excellent idea." Mariah heard Belinda speaking and was happy for her cousin's support.

"And I second that," Shari interjected. Coming from the head of operations for Lillian's of Chicago, it was high praise indeed. "I wish I would have thought of it myself."

"Perhaps Mariah can convince Mr. Myers to consider expanding his interests," Jackson said, glancing over at

Mariah, who colored with embarrassment. She knew her brothers thought that she'd been the driving force behind Everett's decision to partner with them.

"And I would certainly entertain the idea," Shari responded. "As we all would."

Several minutes later, the conference call ended.

"That went great," Chase said.

"Yeah, those Chicago Draysons are seeing that they aren't the only smart ones," Jackson added.

"Why must you always be so negative toward them?" Mariah inquired.

"I agree with Mariah," Chase stated. "We need to make and define our own relationship with our Chicago relatives. We can't let some past beef or grudge with our grandparents over money, a situation we weren't even part of, affect our business. Can you agree to that much, Jack?"

"Fine."

"Trust me, starting off a new business isn't going to be easy and we need all the help we can get," Chase said.

Mariah knew the café would be the boost that the bakery needed to increase sales. The development of the Myers Coffee Roasters café was going much faster than she and her brothers thought. Once they'd given the green light, Everett had several general contractors in, quoting on the work. It was a revolving door at the bakery. He'd also had a contract drafted and signed within days.

Each time a contractor came, Everett was right there with him. He made a point of stopping in to speak to Mariah. Not just to introduce her to whoever was there, but to say hello, see how her day was going or grab a pastry and run. Everett Myers was starting to become a permanent fixture in Mariah's life and she was getting used to seeing him every day. When she didn't, she was in a sour mood.

Jackson commented on it late one night when they were cleaning up the kitchen.

"What are you talking about?" Mariah demanded, even though she knew exactly what he meant. The contractors were finalizing their bids, so there was no reason for Everett to stop by every day as he had been doing.

Jackson scoured her with a disbelieving look. "You know what I'm referring to," he countered. "Myers hasn't been here in a few days and you've been sulking around like someone stole your puppy."

She rolled her eyes at him. "Very funny. My life doesn't revolve around him. If you hadn't noticed, I've been quite busy perfecting a new recipe I've been working on."

Her brother raised an eyebrow. "Oh, yeah, you have been pretty secretive about it. What've you got cooking?"

Mariah shrugged. "I'm not sure. I don't have a name for it yet, but I'm close. And when I'm done, I think it'll put us on the map and have Sweetness Bakery quaking in their boots."

He stepped back. "You're that confident?"

Mariah nodded excitedly. She'd had the idea for a while and finally started working on the dessert at home during her spare time. Not that she had much of it, since the bakery took up most of her day. "I think I'm on to something, Jack."

"Well, don't keep me in suspense. When are you going to let me try it out?"

Mariah smiled devilishly. "Soon. Soon."

"We're here," Everett said, when he pulled his Escalade into a parking space outside Lillian's on Thursday morning. The hotel, the coffee importing business and a chaperoning trip for EJ's school had kept him away from the bakery for nearly a week, so he was excited to see the progress on construction.

He'd brought his top barista, Amber Bernard, with him from his flagship coffeehouse in Pike's Market today. Everett had chosen Amber from his current staff to come work at the bakery and wanted her to meet Mariah.

It also helped that Amber wasn't bad on the eyes, either. She was petite, only five feet two, but her large personality more than made up for what she lacked in height. He felt Amber's easy and lighthearted temperament would suit the bakery and help build the customer base, just as she'd done at the Pike's Market location.

She had long brunette curls, big brown eyes and an infectious smile, while her wardrobe was just as colorful as the lady herself. She favored bohemian type outfits— gauzy patterned shirts, floor-sweeping skirts and flat leather sandals—but as long as she could sell coffee, that was just fine with Everett.

"C'mon, Amber," He unbuckled his seat belt. "I want to show you where you'll be working."

"Sure thing, boss," she replied, and followed him inside.

Mariah was standing at the counter and her smile at seeing him vanished when she realized he wasn't alone, but had a woman with him. "W-who's this?"

Everett saw the flash of jealousy that sparked across Mariah's face when she spotted Amber, and he quite enjoyed it. It meant that she was starting to see him as hers and that secretly thrilled him. "Mariah, I'd like you to meet Amber Bernard, the barista who'll be on-site for Myers Coffee Roasters. Amber, this is Mariah Drayson, the owner of Lillian's of Seattle and the best baker in this town."

He watched the tension ease out of Mariah as she

warmly smiled at Amber and extended her hand. "Nice to meet you."

Instead of accepting the handshake, Amber leaned toward Mariah and gave her a hug. "Great meeting you, as well. I look forward to working with you."

Mariah was obviously surprised by the open display of affection, but returned Amber's hug. "As do I."

"I wanted Amber to come by to meet you," Everett continued, "as well as see where she'll be working."

Mariah turned to her. "Would you like a tour of the bakery?"

Amber smiled back at her. "Love one."

Everett watched the two women walk away without a backward glance at him. "I guess I'll entertain myself?"

Mariah waved a hand behind her and Everett couldn't resist a chuckle.

Without thinking, Mariah circled her arm through Amber's. There was a warm, friendly aura around the barista and Mariah had seen it, felt it as soon as she'd gotten over her momentary pang of jealousy at finding Everett with another woman.

When she'd exited the kitchen and seen him standing there in the storefront, her stomach had lurched and her heart had begun palpitating faster in her chest. She'd missed him, and her body was betraying her by telling her that he was more to her than just a business partner. Seeing him with another woman had felt like a gut punch, because perhaps he didn't feel the same way anymore? Mariah was happy to know that wasn't the case and wanted to welcome Amber to her new workplace.

"How long have you known Everett?" she asked as she led Amber to the back of the building where the offices were located. Unfortunately, Chase had gone to the bank, so she wasn't able to introduce him.

"A couple of years now," Amber replied. "Mr. Myers likes to get know all his employees and routinely drops in on all the coffeehouses."

"Really?" Mariah wouldn't have thought he had the time.

"Yep." Amber nodded. "He really cares about us. And the company offers great benefits. Health insurance and college education assistance."

"Oh, my." Mariah touched her chest. "I hadn't realized. That's very generous."

"That's Mr. Myers."

Mariah was silent as she absorbed the information. He was fast becoming someone she not only liked, but admired and respected for his work ethic.

Amber stared at her strangely for a couple minutes before inquiring, "Are you and Mr. Myers involved?"

Her question startled Mariah. "Why would you ask that?"

She shrugged. "Oh, I don't know…all the sexual tension coming off the both of you."

Mariah didn't have a comeback from that because Amber was right. "Is it that obvious?"

She chuckled. "To me? Yes. I'm pretty good at reading people's auras and you guys are off the charts."

"Well, nothing's happened."

"Not yet," Amber said with a smirk. "But it will."

"How can you be so sure?"

"Oh, I just know."

"Do you?" Mariah paused for several beats before asking, "Why haven't you pursued him yourself?"

"Me and Mr. Myers?" Amber let out a hearty laugh. "Oh, that would never work. I'm too much of a free spirit for Everett. He needs someone more grounded. Plus I admire him big-time and would never ruin that, but he's a great guy. You won't go wrong with him."

Mariah was surprised by Amber's honesty and thoughtful insight. She wasn't sure she was any match for Everett, either, with all her baggage, but the barista seemed certain that a relationship was in the cards for them. "Thank you." Mariah didn't have any friends in Seattle, but something told her that she'd just made one. "Thanks a lot."

She started walking down the hall. "C'mon, let me show you the kitchen."

"This is where all the magic happens?" Amber asked from the doorway.

"That's right," Mariah replied. "I'd like to introduce you to my brother Jackson. Jack…" She motioned him forward.

"Who's this?" he asked, surveying Amber from head to toe.

Mariah rolled her eyes at him. She hoped her brother wasn't about to come on to her. "Jack, this is Amber, our new barista for the café."

His mouth formed an O. "Great to meet you." He wiped his hand on his apron and offered it to her.

She shook it with fervor. Amber didn't seem to care about Jack's dust-splattered apron. "Nice to meet you."

"I've got to check on my focaccia," Jackson said as he began walking backward. "Look forward to working with you." He rushed toward the convection ovens.

When the tour was over, Mariah led Amber back to the front. "That's about it."

As the barista surveyed the baked goods in the display cases, Mariah leaned close to Everett, who'd been waiting for them. "If I could have a word?"

"Sure."

They left Amber in the café area and Mariah led Everett toward the administrative office. Fortunately for her it was empty, because Chase still hadn't returned from his errands.

"As you can see, everything is going smoothly," she said. "We have construction under control, so your visits to the bakery won't be needed and we can limit our association."

Everett frowned and it was clear she'd offended him. She hadn't meant to, but the café was off the ground, so he didn't really need to stop by every day unless—

"Our association is far from over," Everett responded. "In fact, I'd say it's about to heat up."

"Oh, yeah?"

Before she could protest, Everett's arm encircled her waist and he pulled her to him and claimed her lips. It was a surprisingly gentle kiss considering he was angry with her, and Mariah knew she should take a step back, but she didn't, couldn't. All she could do was stand there and let him take over in a kiss so utterly thorough and commanding that her entire being became inflamed. He took his time feasting on her and when he sought out her tongue, she didn't dare pull away. She readily gave it up to him, causing him to draw her closer, tighter into his embrace as he greedily sucked on it.

She hadn't realized just how much she'd hungered for another one of his kisses until now. When he slowly pulled away, Mariah was slightly dazed and barely registered what he said as she inhaled a deep breath and released it.

"Come out with me tomorrow night," Everett stated, rather than asked. "And this time it will be about you and me. Everett and Mariah. Not Myers Coffee Roasters and Lillian's of Seattle. Say yes."

She wanted to resist. "Oh, I don't know…" Her head was still cloudy from his drugging kisses.

He used her uncertainty to seal the deal. "You know you want to," he whispered. "If you need further convincing, I can supply it."

Mariah felt his steady gaze boring into her in silent expectation. She'd felt the heat behind that kiss and knew he had, as well. He wouldn't give up and perhaps she should stop fighting the inevitable. The attraction between them certainly hadn't lessened. "Okay," she finally agreed. "I'll go out with you."

He smiled broadly, clearly pleased that he'd gotten his way. "Good." He bent down to steal another kiss. "Until next time."

Chapter 10

"Big date?" EJ asked Everett from the edge of the bed on Friday night, as he sat in his father's bedroom watching him get ready for an evening with Mariah.

Everett spun around to face him as he patted his cheeks with aftershave. "Yeah, but how do you know?"

EJ shrugged. "I just can tell. You're really happy and smiling a whole lot. I just figured you must really like her."

"And how would you feel about that?" Everett inquired, hiking up his trousers so he could bend down and be at eye level with his son. This was the first time he'd been this excited about a woman since he'd been widowed. But he had to be sure it was right for his son, too.

"I dunno."

Everett couldn't read what his son was thinking. "Yes, you do."

"I want you to be happy. So I guess if she makes you grin like that—" EJ poked his index finger into one of Everett's dimples "—then she can't be half-bad."

"She's not," Everett responded with a smile as he rose to his feet. "And one day soon I'd like you to meet her."

"For real?"

Everett smiled. "For real." He suspected that Mariah Drayson just might become a permanent fixture in his life, so she would need to meet his other half, his son. Everett just hoped she wouldn't have a problem with him having a child. He'd never brought EJ up in their conversations because he'd tried to keep their talks either on business, or light and playful. But tonight was about just the two of them. He was going to have to open up about himself and his past if he ever expected them to go the distance as a couple. And tonight would tell him all he needed to know.

Mariah was ready for her second date with Everett. She'd selected an asymmetrical, snakeskin-print, charmeuse maxi dress with gladiator sandals. She turned around so she could see a side view of her reflection in her bathroom mirror. The paneling spiraled into the shirred, flowing back and showed just enough curves, while the tank style revealed the slight swell of her breasts without being indecent. All in all, she was set for the evening.

Everett had told her to dress "comfortable yet casual" and she thought she'd pulled it off. She hadn't had anything she wanted to wear and had made a quick stop at Nordstrom to find something suitable.

When the doorbell rang, Everett was waiting for her dressed casually in dark trousers, a V-neck sweater and loafers.

He walked toward her as she reached for her shawl and purse. "You look lovely." His eyes raked every inch of her in the charmeuse dress.

"I'm glad you approve," Mariah said as she preceded him out of the building.

"Oh, I do."

Once outside, she noticed the fancy sports car sitting at the curb. "Nice ride," she commented. "You're driving tonight," she added, when he came around to the driver's side and climbed in.

He gave her a sideways glance as he turned on the engine. "I am. I wanted the night to be just the two of us."

Mariah glanced at all the gadgets and dials on the console. "This is quite impressive compared with your Escalade. How long have you had it?"

"Not long." He revved the motor. "I bought it for my thirtieth birthday. This is only my second time taking it out for a spin."

Mariah turned to face him. "If you want to impress me, Everett, you don't have to try so hard."

"I wasn't," he responded, and winked as he took off. "Trust me, if I were, you'd know it. But if I was, how would I be faring?"

She flashed a smile. "Very well indeed."

As they drove, they chatted about their respective days, before venturing on to the latest news topics. Conversation between them was always smooth. They had an easy camaraderie whenever they were together. Mariah didn't have to think of things to say to keep communication moving because Everett was knowledgeable on a variety of topics.

As they neared the Washington Ship Canal, Mariah began to wonder where they were going. The Ballard Locks would be an odd choice for a romantic date. She glanced down at her gladiator sandals. Even with a low heel, she wasn't prepared to stroll through the marina or climb any ladders to watch the salmon pass through the fresh- and saltwater locks.

Everett glanced over at her. "Wondering where we're going?"

"Quite frankly, yes," she admitted. "I'm not exactly dressed for a night at the marina."

He gave a low baritone chuckle and she felt her stomach leap in response. "Don't worry, I wouldn't dream of mussing you up, not since you went to all the trouble of looking good for me."

Mariah's breath hitched in her throat. She wanted to say she hadn't dressed up for him, but it would be a lie. She had and he'd noticed.

Everett stopped the car at the back entrance to the Carl English Botanical Gardens, adjacent to the Ballard Locks, and came around to open her door.

Mariah looked at the setting. "What are we doing here?"

He took her hand. "You'll see."

Everett's touch caused an electrical current to shoot right through her. And when she glanced in his direction, he winked at her. He'd felt it, too, that strange, inexplicable pull whenever they were together. It unnerved her.

An elderly man holding a picnic basket was waiting for them. "Good evening, Mr. Myers."

"Good evening, Joseph. I'd like to introduce you to Mariah Drayson."

"Good evening, madam," the older man said. "Please go inside and enjoy your evening."

Everett patted the man's arm. "Thank you." He took the picnic basket with his free hand, not letting go of Mariah's with the other. He led her through the garden grounds, and they stopped to admire the variety of plants from around the world, including flowering perennials, fan palms, oaks, Mexican pines and rhododendrons. The colors, fragrances and open air helped to awaken Mariah's senses and made her very aware of Everett and his own unique scent.

"Watch your step," he said as he led her off the trail and down a grassy slope.

The sun was setting, but Mariah could still see in front of her, and stopped suddenly, nearly catching Everett off guard. Farther down the hill a picnic area had been set up in front of a small stage with bright lights that illuminated the area. She'd heard about free concerts at the gardens but had never been to one. Except this time, there were no other people around except them.

She turned to Everett. "Did you do all of this?"

He grinned broadly. "I did. I know a few folks who help run the place and…" His voice trailed off.

Once again Everett was impressing her and reminding her that he would go to any lengths to romance her. "This is really special…" It was all she could manage to say as she continued walking down the slope of the romantic English-country setting with him.

When they made it to the blanket, Everett helped her to the ground before settling beside her with the picnic basket.

Mariah rubbed her hands together. "So what have you got in there?" she asked excitedly.

He laughed, "Oh, a little bit of this, a little bit of that."

"Well, let me see." She reached for the basket, but Everett slid it farther away. After growing up with two older brothers, Mariah was not to be outdone and rushed at him, tackling him to the blanket. In so doing, she ended up on top of his hard, lean body. Everett had an inherent masculine strength that oozed from his powerfully built frame and, heaven help her, she couldn't resist him.

They stared at each other for several seconds. Her throat felt tight and constricted and her insides burned hotter than an inferno. In the end, it was Mariah who gave in first and lowered her head. Her lips were hesitant, softly brushing his before becoming more insistent as they moved across his soft mouth. Everett took the bait and rose slightly as one of his hands came around the back of her head, bringing her closer to him so he could deepen the kiss.

It was a slow, languorous kiss and one that had Mariah warring with herself. She'd said that she would keep her distance from Everett, but the second he laid on the charm she was agreeing to a date. And now…now she was kissing him with a hunger and fervor that both surprised and incited her. So when his tongue licked the seam of her lips, demanding entry, she opened them. Greedily, taking his tongue and sucking on it while his hands roamed over her body to her buttocks and cupped her.

She wrapped her arms around his neck and her whole body fell atop him. That's when she felt the bulge in his pants. She'd done that. She'd turned him on with just one kiss. It secretly thrilled her that she could have such an instant effect on him, but why should she be surprised? He'd been doing the same thing to her from the moment they'd met.

"Ahem." A loud cough from above them caused them to pull away.

Everett was the first to recover from the passionate embrace and he spoke without removing his arms from around her waist. "Yes?"

"Sir, we'll be ready to begin in about fifteen minutes," Joseph said, a stone's throw away from them.

"Of course," Everett said smoothly. "Proceed."

Embarrassed at being caught, Mariah moved away and sat upright, straightening her clothes.

"Don't be embarrassed." He turned to her, stretching out on his side, and leaned his head on his elbow. "I enjoyed your spontaneity."

Mariah glanced at him through tremulous lashes. "You did?" She'd never been the aggressor during her marriage to Richard. He'd always been the one to initiate love-making and she'd thought that was normal.

Everett reached across the small space between them and lightly caressed her cheek with the palm of his hand. His eyes were dark and stormy with lust. The very same lust she'd felt moments ago and still felt. "Yes, immensely," he responded.

Everett watched Mariah as she swayed on the blanket to the smooth sounds of Brian McKnight, her favorite singer. She'd been stunned when he'd taken to the stage as they enjoyed a gourmet picnic dinner, and began singing "Cherish."

It had taken a lot of legwork on Everett's part, but he'd succeeded in securing the entertainer for a private concert for just the two of them. And the look on Mariah's face right now told him it had been worth every penny. Her eyes were alight with joy and Everett could see that not only was she enjoying herself, but she was starting to feel comfortable being around him. His slow and steady approach was working. It wasn't easy on his libido, though. Whenever he was around her, it was impossible not to want to take her to his bed and ravish her body all night. He recalled how his manhood had swelled in response to her spontaneous kiss. Even now he desired her, but he would rein it in until Mariah gave the word or a signal that she was ready to take their relationship to the next level.

For him, that meant introducing her to EJ, though he hadn't exactly shared that he had an eight-year-old son. Everett had assumed she would have figured it out when she'd researched him online, but then he realized she didn't know. Probably because he prided himself in keeping EJ's life private from the inquisitive eyes of the press. So he hadn't been forthcoming with the information. It was his job as a parent to protect EJ, and because he hadn't been sure where their relationship would lead, he'd kept the fact of EJ's existence to himself. But tonight gave Everett hope that Mariah could really be a contender as the next woman in his and EJ's life.

At that moment, she turned to him. "Everett, this is incredible," she said. "I can't thank you enough for this." She reached across the small space between them and took his hand and gave it a squeeze.

Everett felt a jolt of electricity run through him at her tender touch. "You're welcome."

When Brian McKnight began singing one of his popular love songs, "Love of My Life," Everett rose to his feet. "Would you like to dance?"

"Absolutely."

And that's how they continued the remainder of the evening—in each other's arms swaying to the smooth grooves. When he returned Mariah to her apartment nearly two hours later, he switched the car engine off and they sat for several long, excruciating moments. Did she not want the night to end, either?

He'd never considered himself a die-hard romantic, but the evening was made for lovers, with the music, the picnic with champagne, caviar and the stars overhead. But he wouldn't push, not until she was ready.

Mariah turned to face him. He couldn't see what she was thinking because it was too dark in the car's interior, but he could tell she was warring with herself. "Everett, I…"

"Yes?" He encouraged her to say whatever she was thinking, feeling.

She took her time, as if formulating her thoughts. "I don't think I've ever had such a great time like I did tonight. I didn't think you could top the Space Needle, but you did. This was truly the best date ever!"

Everett beamed with pride. "Thank you and you're welcome." He suspected there was something else on her mind and he waited for her to say more.

"Th-this isn't easy for me," Mariah stammered, wringing her hands. "You and me." She pointed to his chest and then hers.

"I know."

"You've been very patient and I'm sorry if I've given you mixed signals. I—I just wasn't sure I was ready to dive into another relationship after my divorce."

"And now?" he asked quietly.

"I can't deny the feelings I have toward you are growing, and I guess what I'm saying very ineffectually is that I'd like to pursue them and see where this goes. I won't fight you anymore."

If he could have jumped up and down, Everett would have. He knew how much that admission had cost her. So he treaded lightly and reached for her hands in the darkened space and clasped them. "Thank you for being honest with me and yourself." He smiled. "And this relationship can move as slow or as fast as you need it to, without any pressure from me."

"You mean that?"

He chuckled. If he was reading her correctly, she must have expected him to make a move on her so he could take her to bed tonight. And with any other woman, he might have, but not Mariah. She was special and a little bit delicate, so for now he would treat her like the princess she was. But when the time came for them to become lovers, he would unleash his desires. "Of course I do," he murmured. "Let me walk you inside."

They ended the evening at her doorstep, wrapped up in each other arms. And this time Mariah didn't resist his kisses. Instead she was a full participant, coaxing his lips apart with her tongue and diving inside to mate it with his. The kiss was like soldering heat that joined metals, and they fused together as one.

Everett erupted with desire and returned her ardor by covering her mouth with hungry kisses. Mariah gave herself freely up to the passion of his embrace, and when then finally separated, he caressed her cheek and said, "Good night, sweetheart."

As her apartment door closed, Everett realized that he was falling hard for the sexy baker. Which meant that now was the time. She had to pass one final test. It was time she met EJ.

Chapter 11

Mariah continued tinkering with the recipe for her new creation on Saturday morning at the bakery. She always tried to keep busy when her mind was preoccupied, and it was, thanks to her new relationship with Everett. She'd agreed to date him and see where it would lead. In the light of day, however, she was having cold feet.

What did she know about dating, anyway? Her experience was severely limited because she'd gotten married so young. And Everett, well, he was a grown man with a man's needs, and she had grave reservations about taking their relationship to the next level, in the bedroom.

She was sure a man of Everett's stature and reputation had been with many women since his wife's passing. Mariah had resisted the urge to find out more online, other than his business interests. She hadn't wanted to know how she compared to other women he saw, or his deceased wife, all of whom were probably more sophisticated than she.

She knew he'd been married and lost his wife, but reading any more about that loss would have been too personal and too intrusive. Mariah hadn't felt right reading about Everett's greatest tragedy.

So she'd decided to come to the bakery and perfect her creation once and for all. And she had. She'd also finally come up with a name for it, and consequently had woken up both her brothers to meet her at the bakery at 5:00 a.m. Jackson was used to being up so early, while Chase, a numbers man, didn't normally stop by the bakery until much later.

Needless to say, Chase came in bleary-eyed, wearing sweatpants and a T-shirt. "What's so urgent?" he inquired. "That you had to wake me from my peaceful sleep?"

Jackson shrugged. "I was already on my way, so it makes no difference to me. What you got, kid?" He was dressed for the day in dark denims and a fitted muscle shirt.

Mariah ignored both of them and held up her creation. "I have come up with the next great pastry." She lifted the covered platter. "I give you…the Draynut!" She removed the lid and presented her work with a flourish.

"What is it?" Chase asked, looking up at her. "It looks like a doughnut, but…" He stared at it as if it was a foreign object.

Mariah sighed wearily. "Just try it." She held out the platter, and reluctantly Chase and Jackson each withdrew a pastry and sampled it.

"Mmm…" was all Mariah heard from both of them after they'd taken their first bite.

"This is delicious, sis," Jackson responded, reaching for a second one. "What'd you put in it?"

She smiled wickedly. "I'll never tell. Matter-of-fact, I want to trademark this recipe and name immediately.

Chase, that's where I need your help. I want to ensure no one gets their hands on this and tries to replicate it. The secret ingredients need to be kept under lock and key."

Jackson seemed affronted, but kept eating his Draynut. "Even from me?"

"It's nothing personal," Mariah said. "But I think you can agree we have something great here, and for the moment I'd like to keep it close to the vest."

Chase reached for a paper towel from the nearby counter and wiped his mouth, because he'd already finished his sample. "I agree we don't want anyone else to get their hands on this, so you will need to give me the recipe for the trademark."

"When you have all the paperwork ready, let me know," Mariah said. "In the meantime, we should debut the Draynut at the grand opening of Myers Coffee Roasters café. I've already prepared a press release."

She held up the document she'd spent most of last night preparing, because she'd tossed and turned in bed after Everett had dropped her off, until finally giving up and coming to the bakery.

"Let me see that." Jackson read the one-pager. When he was done, he handed it to Chase. "That's really good, Mariah. You're doing some spectacular work, kid. Who knew you had it in you?"

Mariah smiled. She knew that Jackson's back-handed compliment was meant with love and affection. "Thanks, bro."

Chase turned to them both after he was done reading the press release. "Well done, Mariah, well done. What price point did you have in my mind for the Draynut?"

"I don't know. Maybe three dollars?"

"Too low," Jackson declared. "We need to go higher. This is a specialty item and the more expensive it is, the higher in demand it will become. Look at what happened with the Cronut phase in New York. Let's charge five dollars like they did."

Chase pointed his finger at his brother. "Jack has a point, Mariah. This—" he held up the platter of Draynuts "—is a gold mine and we want everyone to know that, like you said, it's the next best thing!"

Mariah smiled warmly. She was thrilled that her brothers were just as excited as she was by her new creation. "Let's do it!"

Later that evening, Mariah scooted out early from the bakery. They'd hired an intern. Kelsey Andrews was a cute blonde with short curly hair, a petite figure and gorgeous hazel eyes. She was working a few hours during their peak times and helping them at the cash register. It allowed Mariah a few hours off during the week to run errands, or in today's case, take a break.

She was meeting up with Amber at what looked to be an after-school center, she thought, as she drove up to the one-story building. The two women had hit it off after their first meeting, exchanged phone numbers and agreed to get together. Though Mariah had no idea that this was what Amber did in her spare time.

She was waiting outside by the curb as Mariah pulled up. "Thanks for the ride," Amber said as she got in. "My red Bug is giving me car trouble. I'd love to get rid of it, but I've had it for years.

"It's no problem," Mariah replied. "So, what do you do at the center?"

"I work with preteen girls as part of a group that fosters girl empowerment."

"That's wonderful."

"They're always looking for volunteers. You should

think about it. After a background check, you could qualify to help out these young girls. Just let me know if you're interested."

Mariah glanced at the school as she drove away. She wasn't sure she could be around small kids consistently, knowing she couldn't have one of her own. But then again, maybe it would be cathartic? Helping children might ease her own pain and loss.

"What's wrong?" Amber's warm brown eyes were staring at her.

She shrugged. "It's nothing."

"It's more than that," Amber replied. "There's a sadness in your eyes that wasn't there before I started talking about my work."

Mariah changed the subject. "How about a cocktail first?"

Once they'd arrived at a popular wine room, filled their wine cards with money and used them to help dispense the ounces of wine they wanted, they settled into two large, comfy leather chairs to chat and get to know each other.

Mariah learned Amber's family was originally from the South, but had migrated north. She was attending graduate school at the University of Washington and getting her masters of business degree.

"And in my spare time I'm an artist. Well, more like a jewelry maker, to be exact." Amber held out her wrists so Mariah could see the bracelets she wore, and then pointed to her ears and neck to showcase the matching earrings and necklace.

"Do you sleep?" Mariah asked, sipping her merlot. "Or maybe cure world hunger?" She laughed at her own joke.

And so did Amber. "I don't know." She shrugged. "I just like to keep busy. And as far as my jewelry—" she held up her wrists again and admired her adornments "—I've always loved making them and would love to sell them full-time."

"Then you should," Mariah said. "I for one would certainly buy them. I love the necklace you're wearing." She reached out to finger the different stones and beadwork on the chain dangling from Amber's slender neck.

Her new friend beamed and a smile spread across her lips. "Thank you. And I'll bring some of my pieces next time to the bakery so you can take a look."

"I would love that."

"But enough about me. Why don't you tell me what got you so down earlier?"

Mariah shrugged.

"C'mon. I know we're not best friends or anything, but I'd like to be an ear to listen." Amber slid her legs underneath her on the chair and faced Mariah.

Mariah mulled it over. What could it hurt to confide in Amber? It would be nice to have a sounding board, especially with Belinda so far away in Chicago. "All right, it's really quite simple. I can't have children," she blurted out. Sometimes it was better to rip off a Band-Aid rather than ease it off.

Amber was silent for a long moment. "And how does that make you feel?"

"Damaged. Diminished. Less than a woman. All of the above." Mariah took a gulp of her wine. She'd never been this blunt and honest with anyone before and shared her deepest thoughts, but something told her she could trust Amber.

Amber reached across the distance between them and squeezed her hand. "I know I can't tell you how to feel about it, but you're *still* an amazing woman and that hasn't changed. And whether or not you're physically able to birth a child, you can still be a mother. There are so many children in need out there who would be lucky to have a mom like you."

Mariah smiled at Amber with tears in her eyes. "Thank you, thank you. I think I needed to hear that. It's been hard having this hanging over my head. My infertility and my quest to get pregnant destroyed my marriage, and I fear it could do the same thing again."

"With Everett?"

She glanced at Amber. "How did you know?"

Amber laughed softly. "How could I not? The chemistry was coming off you two in droves when we met. I'd have to be blind not to see how into you he is. But I take it he doesn't know?"

Mariah nodded and drank more of her wine. "It's not exactly a topic of conversation you dive right into when you're getting to know someone, but if things progress between us…"

"You'll tell him," Amber said. "When you're ready. And when you do, I'll be there to support you."

"Thanks, Amber. I have to tell you that I really needed a friend here in Seattle and I'm really happy to have met you. I sure could have used you a year ago in Chicago," she said with a laugh.

"Well, I'm here now and feel free to lean on me."

"Oh, I will," Mariah stated emphatically. "I will. And you can do the same."

It was Sunday morning and Everett felt he deserved a treat for all his hard work, such as a pastry at Lillian's after he'd completed his usual weekend workout in his home gym. As he dressed in distressed jeans and a polo shirt, he knew the real reason he was going. He wanted to see Mariah.

Now that she'd agreed to date him, Everett didn't have

to make excuses to see her anymore. He could visit the bakery any time he wanted.

Except today was different. This time he was bringing EJ with him so he could finally introduce his son to the lady in his life. Everett had to admit that he was a little nervous at the prospect. He had no idea how EJ would respond to having another person, a woman, in his father's life. He might see her as an interloper in their relationship, and things could go badly.

On the other hand, EJ might like Mariah, which would please Everett immensely, because he so desperately wanted his son to like her as much as he did. There might not be a future if she wasn't receptive to his having a child. Everett knew it wasn't fair that he was springing EJ on her this way without any warning, but the right moment to tell her had never arisen.

Everett had spent the last four weeks trying to break through the wall and electrified fence Mariah had erected around her heart. Friday night had been the first time he'd felt comfortable enough to share his past, but the evening had been so romantic Everett hadn't had the heart to ruin it. Yesterday, after their date, he'd given some serious thought to whether or not Mariah was ready to meet EJ. He'd then decided it was time, and today was the day. Mariah might become angry with him due to his lack of forthrightness. So he'd kept EJ's existence to himself, but not anymore.

Today, Mariah would meet the most important person in Everett's life. He just prayed that EJ would become as important to her as he was to him.

EJ was waiting for him at the breakfast bar, already dressed for the day in jeans, a print T-shirt and sneakers. He looked like a mini version of Everett except he had a headful of curly hair, while Everett's hair was clipped short.

"Morning, Dad."

"Good morning, EJ," Everett said, on his way to his Keurig coffee maker. He inserted a K-cup and placed a mug underneath from the cupboard. The coffee percolated and was ready within minutes. "What are we doing today, Dad?" EJ asked.

"I thought we could stop by a bakery and grab a snack."

"We normally have a big breakfast on Saturday," EJ complained with a frown.

"I know," Everett said, sipping his coffee. "But I want us to try something different. Plus I want you to see the new location Daddy's been working on. You all right with that?"

"Sure," EJ said. "Guess so."

After he'd finished his coffee, Everett and EJ set off for Lillian's of Seattle. Traffic was light and they made it to the Denny Triangle section of downtown Seattle in no time. When he opened the door, the bakery was bustling with Sunday visitors getting a snack or picking up a birthday cake. While in line, he could hear patrons commenting about what was going on behind the temporary door they'd hung to keep the construction apart from the customers. He noticed Mariah was remaining mum at the register.

Everett had to admit that even with her honey-blond hair piled in a simple updo and very little makeup on, as usual, she still was the most beautiful woman in the room.

When the crowd began to dissipate, she finally looked up and noticed Everett and EJ in line. "Everett," she exclaimed, tucking her hair into place and smoothing her apron. "What are you doing here?"

He smiled as he placed his hands on EJ's shoulders

and walked him toward the counter. She was right to be surprised. He hardly ever came in on weekends since he spent most of them with his son. But today was different.

She smiled down at EJ. "And who do you have with you?"

"Mariah, I'd like you to meet my son."

Chapter 12

Mariah stared back at Everett, dumbfounded. Had she heard him correctly? Had he really said *his son*? She looked at Everett and then at the young boy at his side and had her answer. He looked exactly like Everett, just a miniature version. With wooden legs, she walked from behind the counter to greet him.

She bent down until she was the boy's height. "It's nice to meet you, EJ." She extended her hand. "Finally." She glanced up at Everett and could swear she saw him sweating bullets.

"Nice to meet you, too, Miss Mariah."

Mariah smiled into his endearing brown eyes and melted. He'd called her Miss Mariah. She'd never thought she'd hear a child say her name.

Mariah rose to her feet. "You hungry? We have some blueberry muffins that just came out of the oven."

EJ wrinkled his nose. "I don't like blueberries."

Mariah chuckled at his honesty. "How about chocolate chip? Will that do?"

A broad smile came across his small features as he nodded.

"C'mon." She held out her hand. "Follow me."

EJ started toward her and then glanced behind him at his father.

Everett nodded. "It's okay. Go ahead."

So EJ grasped her hand and walked with her toward the kitchen. Mariah couldn't resist a backward scouring look at Everett as they departed.

But once they made it to the kitchen, she was all smiles as she showed EJ around.

"Who do we have here?" Jackson asked as they approached the cooling table bearing a batch of chocolate chip muffins just out of the oven.

"This is EJ." Mariah lifted the boy onto a stool, then went in search of a plate.

"What's your full name, little fella?" Jackson inquired.

"EJ Myers."

"Is that short for Everett Myers Jr.?" Jackson glanced in Mariah's direction as she returned with a paper plate.

EJ nodded. "Yep, I'm named after my dad."

"And that's a very strong name indeed." Mariah reached for one of the muffins, placed it on the plate and slid it over to EJ.

"Thank you, Miss Mariah," he said, right before he grabbed the muffin and took a generous bite. Since it was still warm, the chocolate chips inside were a bit gooey and were now all over his face.

Mariah laughed as she walked to the paper towel rack hanging from the wall and ripped off a piece. "Here, wipe your face."

EJ accepted the paper towel but didn't use it. Instead, he bit into the muffin again.

"So," Jackson whispered, coming toward her. "You're just meeting EJ?"

Mariah didn't get a chance to answer before EJ did, with a mouthful of muffin. "Yep, my dad said it was time that I meet someone special because we might be spending a lot of time together."

Mariah's heart instantly warmed at EJ's continued honesty. It was so refreshing and revealing. How could she be mad at Everett when he'd told his son that she was someone special and he wanted them to get to know each other? It was clear to her that Everett saw potential in their relationship. Why else would he introduce her to his son? Otherwise, he would have continued to keep EJ's existence a secret, as he'd done for a month.

Of course, she was still upset with him on that front. Because although she understood his reasoning, he still should have told her he had a son. He hadn't introduced them because he hadn't known where their relationship would lead, but to blindside her? That wasn't cool and she intended to tell him so.

"Jack, can you watch EJ for a moment while I go speak with his father?"

"Absolutely," her brother said with a smile. He knew what Everett had in store.

"Be right back." Mariah squeezed EJ's shoulder before she exited the room. "You'll be in good hands with my brother."

"Okay." EJ was oblivious to her as he continued devouring the muffin.

Mariah passed by Kelsey, who was tending to the front of the house, and found Everett behind the wooden partition, in the café. There was no construction during the weekend, so it was just the two of them. As excited as she was at the prospect of Myers Coffee Roasters café opening and the debut of Lillian's of Seattle's Draynut, it was time Mr. Myers got a talking to.

The look on her face must have been a dead giveaway to her mood because Everett instantly stepped back when she entered the small area. He offered her a weak smile.

"Why didn't you tell me about EJ?" She wasted no time getting to the point.

"I know you're upset—"

"Darn right, I'm upset," Mariah said, folding her arms across her chest. "A child? A *child*? How could you keep something as important as your child to yourself?"

Everett sighed. "It's precisely for that reason that I did." Mariah snorted, but he continued. "When I first started visiting, you were adamant that you weren't interested in getting to know me."

"That doesn't make it right."

"I know that and I agree, but you have to understand my point of view as a parent. The parent of a child who has already experienced more loss than any child should, the loss of his mother. I didn't want to bring someone into his life who wasn't going to be sticking around. It wouldn't be fair. I made the choice and I stand behind it, but I will agree that I should have at least told you about EJ's existence. I guess I figured when you'd looked me up online that websites would have mentioned him."

She shook her head. "There's nothing about EJ online. You've done a good job of shielding him from the press, given the circumstances, and that should be commended."

"Thank you. So I take it you don't know much about Sara, his mother?"

Mariah shrugged. "I didn't read up on your deceased wife or the accident. It felt kind of morbid, as well as deeply personal. I didn't think I had the right. I guess I figured you'd tell me when you were ready."

Everett was introspective for several long moments, making Mariah wonder if she shouldn't have mentioned his wife. Were the memories still too painful even after five years? When he finally spoke his voice was soft. "Thank you for your sensitivity. I'd like to talk to you about it one day. But for now, it's just important that you and EJ get to know each other. He's never really had a female presence in his life other than my mother and Margaret, our housekeeper."

Mariah couldn't stay mad at Everett, not when he'd done it to protect his son. She walked over to him, pulled him close and hugged him for several long moments. Shifting slightly, she held his face with both hands and stared deep into his dark eyes. "Thank you for thinking me worthy of meeting EJ. I'm honored."

And without thinking, she kissed him square on the lips, not caring where they were or who might walk in and see them making out. His mouth moved over hers, devouring its softness, and she parted her lips so he could deepen the kiss. Mariah felt spirals of ecstasy radiating through her entire body and knew they'd turned a corner.

"Ahem, ahem." A knock on the wooden door showed Jackson at the entry with EJ at his knees. "Someone was looking for you. Said he's still hungry after the chocolate chip muffin."

Mariah and Everett separated, but he kept his arm wrapped around her waist. "How about some lunch?" he inquired, glancing sideways at her.

Mariah looked down at her watch. She was tempted, but it was just past eleven and she really should stay and work. "It's a bit early—"

"Don't worry, sis," Jackson said from the door. "Kelsey and I can handle the bakery until you get back."

Her face split into a grin. "All right." She slid from Everett's embrace and untied her apron. "What do you say, EJ?" She walked toward him. "Can I come, too?"

EJ looked at his father pleadingly.

"Of course she can come," Everett said. "C'mon." And together, the three of them left the bakery.

They ended up at a restaurant known for its breakfast and brunch offerings. Mariah settled into a booth with EJ and his son. As she sat across from them, she was a bit disconcerted. Everett having a son was an unexpected wrinkle in her agreement to date him. Although not unwelcome, it was certainly a game changer.

"So what would you like to eat?" Mariah asked EJ. It amazed her at how much he looked like Everett. He shared his nose and deep-set eyes.

"Pancakes!"

"Pancakes sound great," Mariah exclaimed. "And I make the best. Someday I'll have to fix you some." She glanced at Everett and he smiled, telling her it was indeed a possibility.

"You do? So does Daddy," EJ said. "Did you learn from him?"

Mariah chuckled. "No, from my mother."

"Oh." EJ frowned as if she'd just said something distasteful.

Mariah glanced up at Everett, her eyes filling with concern.

"I'll teach you how to make them," Everett said softly. "And now Miss Mariah can help, too? If she's interested?"

Mariah saw that Everett was worried after EJ's response to her mother comment. Did he expect her to run away because he had a child? She'd been hurt that he hadn't felt he could tell her about EJ from the beginning, but she understood his reasoning and would try to put it behind them.

"Absolutely," she said with a smile. "And perhaps we'll have some bacon and eggs with our pancakes. What do you say, EJ?" When the young boy nodded fervently, she looked at his father. "And what about you, Everett?" She hoped her ease with EJ would alleviate his fears.

"Um…I need some protein after my workout this morning."

Mariah eyed him while he looked at his menu. His personal training would explain his excellent physique. There was no flab on the man, nothing but a lean body. She'd felt his masculine strength every time they'd kissed and it caused sexual tension to prickle inside her.

"Mariah, the waitress was asking you for your order." Everett interrupted her thoughts. "I already placed mine, of steak and eggs."

She glanced up and saw the waitress standing at their booth with a notepad. After rattling off her order, Mariah returned her focus to EJ. "So what are you guys doing today?"

"Clothes shopping," Everett answered. "This boy is growing like a weed. I can't keep him in clothes. I think he's going through a growth spurt."

EJ frowned. "I hate shopping."

"So do I," she said.

EJ seemed surprised. "You do? I thought all girls liked shopping."

Mariah chuckled. "Most do, but I'm with you. It's rather boring. The best part is when it's over."

EJ laughed at her joke and Mariah glanced up to find Everett watching her closely. She hoped he knew that meeting EJ wasn't a deal breaker, so she said, "I'm so happy to finally meet you, EJ. Maybe we can hang out sometime?"

His son offered her a grin. "I'd like that."

Mariah's heart melted on the spot for yet another Myers man.

When she returned from lunch with Everett and EJ, Mariah was contemplative as she walked into the kitchen.

"Well, how did it go?" Jackson inquired. "Don't leave me in suspense."

Mariah grinned. "It went great. Because we were early, we missed the lunch rush."

"I couldn't care less about that. I want to know how you fared with EJ."

Mariah stared up at the ceiling and her mind drifted off to another time. A time when she'd wanted kids so badly she'd have done anything to have one. Tried anything. And she had. She'd quit her job. She'd eaten better. All in her effort to become a mother. And now, when she hadn't been looking for it, it may just have landed in her lap. "It was wonderful."

"You sound surprised," Jackson said. "You've always been good with children, Mariah. Even when we were teenagers, you had a way with them. You'd babysit and they'd actually listen to you. It was like you were the child whisperer or something."

Mariah couldn't suppress her laughter. "The child whisperer?"

"It's true. I bet you charmed the pants off Everett's son."

She hazarded a glance in her brother's direction. "I think I did, but I guess I'll find out, if Everett never calls me again."

Jackson chuckled drily. "Like that would ever happen.

You've had that man sprung from the moment he laid eyes on you."

Mariah blushed. It had been the same for her. She'd thought Everett was attractive at the grand opening, but she'd been too afraid to allow herself to feel anything. Yet she had in time and it was more than she ever could have imagined. Now if their relationship continued to flourish, she had the possibility of a family.

"So, what did you think of Miss Mariah?" Everett asked EJ on the ride home after their brunch as they drove to the mall.

"I like her," EJ replied.

"You do?" To say he was happy was an understatement.

"Yeah, she's really nice and I love her muffins," EJ said, taking off the light jacket he'd been wearing. "Is that why you always bring back pastries to the house?"

"Partially," he responded. "Now that I'm going to have a café there, Dad's going to have to visit often. How do you feel about that?"

"Will we still get a chance to see Miss Amber?"

Everett smiled, remembering how well EJ and the barista had hit it off. "Actually, you will," he responded. "Amber's going to be working at the bakery with Miss Mariah."

"Awesome!" EJ said, and glanced out the window.

Everett stared at him for several seconds before returning his attention to the road. EJ was taking the fact that he was starting to date again really well. He'd always said that he wasn't dating because of EJ, but his son was just fine. Had Everett been the one too scared to take a risk and meet someone new? Or maybe it had just taken the right woman to open up his heart to the prospect?

That woman was Mariah Drayson. And knowing that

she and EJ connected made Everett realize that he was ready to take their relationship to the next level. Every time they were together he'd been reining in his passion and desire for Mariah. Waiting for EJ's blessing? Perhaps. But now that that hurdle was past them, Everett didn't see any reason to hold back any longer.

He wanted to *be* with Mariah in every sense of the word. He wanted to wrap her in his arms, have her legs twine around his waist and lose himself in her sweet heat. To that end, he would arrange a romantic getaway, one that would make it very clear to Mariah exactly what was in store.

"Yes, that sounds lovely. Can't wait," Mariah said, ending the call as she leaned back at her desk in the back of the bakery several days later.

"Is everything all right?" Amber inquired from the doorway. She'd stopped by to see if Mariah had time for lunch because she had a few hours between class and when she was due at the after-school center.

Mariah blinked several times. The conversation she'd just shared with Everett had butterflies jumping around in her stomach. "Yes, yes, I'm fine."

"You don't look like it," Amber replied. "I'll go grab you a glass of water."

"No, no." Mariah didn't want her nosy brothers checking up on her. She rose from the executive chair and pulled Amber inside her office before closing the door. Chase and Jackson were both too intuitive and could always pick up when something or someone was bothering her. She'd never been able to keep things a secret from them, but in this instance she must, because it was about her personal life and she didn't want or need their interference.

"What's going on?" Amber looked at her warily.

Mariah sighed. "I need some advice."

"What kind of advice?"

"About me and Everett."

Amber smiled. "Who else?" she she said with a laugh. "What's going on?"

"Well, he's asked me to join him for a trip to Bainbridge Island.

"That sounds wonderful," Amber gushed. "They have the greatest shops and nifty arts and crafts stores. When I go there…" She paused when she saw Mariah's face. "Sorry, I guess you were talking about you. Go ahead."

"I love the island, too, but he made sure to mention it would be an *overnight* trip," Mariah whispered, as if her brothers had their ears pressed to the door and could hear every word.

"And is this your first *overnight trip*?" Amber asked, her voice rising slightly.

Mariah nodded.

"Oh, my." Amber's cheeks became stained with red.

"I don't mean ever," Mariah responded, "but I don't have a lot of experience in that department."

"Who's to say he does?"

"Have you looked at him?" Mariah inquired with a raised brow. "Haven't you noticed the way women look at him when he walks into a room?"

Amber shrugged. "Probably not, because he's always been my boss. But anyway, I'm sure it's like riding a bike. It'll all come back to you."

Mariah began pacing the floor. "I'm sure it will, but…"

"But nothing, I'm certain that Everett, being the sort of take-charge man that he is, will teach you all you need to know. Don't worry. Just enjoy the moment and let nature take its course."

Mariah smiled. "Thank you, Amber."

"Anytime."

After she'd left, Mariah tried to remember Amber's advice. Everett was a singularly focused, determined man, and clearly he was hoping they would become intimate during this getaway. A brief shiver went up Mariah's spine. It wasn't as if she didn't want him, hadn't wanted him. She'd just been too afraid to make any sort of moves other than a kiss. But Everett had plans now. This time, she wouldn't resist him, and they'd finally become lovers.

Chapter 13

Mariah allowed the wind to ripple through her wavy hair as she and Everett stood on the ferry to Bainbridge Island on Saturday morning. They'd parked the car and walked over to the deck railing so they could take in the scenery. It was only a thirty-five minute ride to the island, but from the boat she could see the snowcapped Olympic Mountains, Seattle's skyline and a view of Mount Rainier. Everett had dropped EJ off with his parents so they could have the day to themselves.

"Isn't it wonderful?" Everett asked, coming behind her and placing his hands on the rail, effectively blocking her inside his embrace.

"Oh, yes," Mariah said. She could feel the heat emanating from the wool jacket he wore and it surrounded her like a warm blanket. Or perhaps it was the smell of his masculine cologne that wafted to her nose? Either way, she was very aware of the man, the trip and all that it represented.

He hadn't said anything when he'd picked up her small suitcase and placed it in the trunk next to his an hour ago, but it was clear they both knew what this night meant.

Mariah, however, was a bundle of nerves and shivered from the cool wind whipping across the bay.

"I thought we could take in a winery," Everett said, when she finally turned around to face him and he wrapped his strong arms around her. "Or the distillery. Whatever you want, this day is yours."

"It's ours," Mariah said, standing on her tippy toes to brush her lips across his.

Everett didn't react at first and Mariah thought that he didn't like a public display of affection. But then those massive hands of his grabbed both sides of her face and he deepened the kiss. Without thinking, she opened her mouth and his tongue slid inside, circling with hers in a deliciously slow mating ritual as they each tasted the other.

When they separated, they took in ragged, deep breaths to fill their lungs with the oxygen they'd just been deprived of after trying to swallow each other whole. Everett was right about one thing. It was time.

Bainbridge Island was a local favorite on the weekends, so the streets of the quaint downtown area were bustling with people walking, talking, or moseying through the shops, eateries and coffee spots. After parking in a public garage, Mariah and Everett walked hand in hand through the town, browsing.

It had been months since Mariah had a day off and she felt guilty leaving Chase and Jackson when the bakery was still so new, but she needed this. Not just for physical reasons, even though she'd been working sixty-hour weeks, but for emotional reasons, too. Whenever she was around Everett she thought she might combust, and she needed a release.

The failure of her marriage had been a blow to her self-esteem. Afterward, she'd felt ugly and unlovable, not to mention heavy from the extra couple pounds she'd gained from stress eating after the divorce. Thanks to those long hours on her feet at the bakery, she'd lost all the weight she'd put on postdivorce, and then some.

Now, when she saw herself through Everett's eyes, she felt sexy. It was heady stuff. They should sell it in the nearest Walgreens or CVS Pharmacy.

Eventually, she and Everett stopped at one of the wineries for a tasting and tried several different wines, from cabernet sauvignon to chardonnay to pinot noir to malbec, all the while laughing and talking. Mariah was learning more and more about what made Everett tick and he discovered that although she had a lot of love from her father, it wasn't the case with her mother.

"Are you sad about that?" Everett inquired.

Mariah shrugged. "Would I like to have one of those TV sitcom relationships with my mother and go to her with my problems? Yes, but that's never been the basis of our relationship. It's always been my dad."

Everett grinned. "A true daddy's girl."

She grinned. "And proud of it."

After lazily drifting through the shops and stores, Mariah and Everett eventually drove to the quaint inn he had chosen. Right away she was struck by the unique architectural details throughout, such as its thatched roof and crown molding. The room the innkeeper led them to was bright and sunny thanks to large bay windows and French doors leading out to a beautiful deck with a view of the water, but it was also elegantly decorated in warm yellow and blues. It housed a large brick fireplace, a cozy sitting area with wicker furniture, and a massive four-poster bed that would easily fit the two of them.

"I hope you enjoy your stay," the woman said as she left.

Once the door closed, Mariah was nervous as to what to do next. She'd never stayed with a man in a hotel room, other than her husband.

But Everett made her feel at ease. "How about we get ready for dinner?" he said, placing her small suitcase on the bed. "If you like, you can use the shower first."

"Thank you, I'd like that."

When she emerged twenty minutes later in one of the fluffy white bathrobes waiting in the master bath, Mariah found the room empty. Everett was standing on the deck watching the sunset.

He didn't hear her as she approached, allowing her the chance to study him closely. He was a fine looking man. His muscled body in the loose-fitting jeans and polo shirt told her he was at ease in whatever he wore. Mariah was attracted to his confidence and wished she had more herself.

She'd taken an extra amount of time in the bath, ensuring she'd showered, shaved and shined enough to entice a man like Everett. She'd moisturized her skin with a fragrant Bath and Body Works lotion and spritzed perfume all over her.

He must have sensed her presence, and turned around. He didn't speak at first, just surveyed her from where he stood.

Barefoot and free of makeup, wearing a plush robe that was likely covering her naked body, Mariah paused in the doorway. Everett groaned inwardly. He heard the voice in his head that warned him to take things slow and make the night romantic by sweeping her off her feet. He blatantly ignored his own edict and instead decided to go for what he wanted more than anything, which was to take her to bed.

Slowly, he walked toward her, closing the French doors behind him, but never taking his eyes off hers. Mariah retreated and edged farther into the room, away from him. Everett couldn't quite make out the emotion reflected in those brown depths, but he intended to find out now.

He backed Mariah up until her legs were pressed against the king-size bed and there was no space between them. No place for her to run. One of his hands came up to caress her and he palmed her face with his hand. "You are so beautiful." She looked downward when he said it, but he lifted her chin. "I mean it. You are. And I'm going to show you just how much."

He reached between them and, grasping the belt of her robe, tugged it free until it fell open. Mariah's gasp at his audacity was audible, but she didn't say a word.

He took that as his cue and, using both hands, slid the robe from her body. It fell to the floor, baring all of her to his admiring gaze.

Everett's eyes roamed, taking in everything—the full swell of her breasts, her flat stomach, the curve of her hips and the triangular patch of curls that awaited him. But it was her up-tilting breasts that he wanted to sample. He'd been aching to touch, to taste, to pleasure them with his hands, his mouth and his tongue. He groaned. He could no longer help himself and lowered his head to take one in his mouth, while his arm curved around Mariah's waist so he could caress her bare bottom.

He took the nipple fully into his heated mouth and suckled, gently at first and then with long greedy pulls. His free hand moved to cup and tease the other breast with his fingers. He wanted everything all at the same time and Mariah didn't deny him.

"Everett," she moaned weakly when he switched to the second breast, claiming it with his lips, teeth and tongue. Over and over, he teased the sensitive bud, laving it with his tongue. He could see he was driving her mad with passion because she was moving against him, pressing to get closer to him.

He wanted to be just as close and swiftly lifted her into his arms and laid her on the bed. Before joining her, he disposed of his shoes, shirt and jeans, until he was standing only in his briefs. Everett knew he had to slow down the pace, otherwise, he'd have her legs in the air and be plunging inside her without making the moment last. He reminded himself to stay in control, until Mariah opened her arms to him, welcoming him into the bed. That's when Everett knew that keeping control would be a hard battle to win.

Mariah couldn't believe how Everett made her feel just by caressing and sucking her breasts. She was on fire from his kisses and caresses. The juncture between her thighs was already starting to ache unbearably. She'd never felt this kind of passion before. Never wanted to be taken, possessed, as she did by Everett in this moment.

As Everett undressed, removing each layer of clothing, Mariah's passion and desire for him grew. His broad shoulders were bare now, showing her the muscled chest she'd felt each time he'd held her when he'd hugged her goodbye. The rest of him was even better. His abdomen was taut and well-defined, his legs long and muscular, and the bulge in the black briefs he wore quite impressive.

Mariah swallowed. She sorely hoped he wouldn't be upset by her lack of experience. Her ex-husband hadn't been one to try more than a few basic positions and Mariah had deferred to him in that department. But now she was eager to please Everett and be a good lover.

And when he joined her on the bed and she felt the weight of his body, nothing else mattered except the two of them in this moment. He slid his arms underneath her, pulling her closer, and then kissed her softly, gently, reverently, and Mariah melted in his embrace.

While his lips traveled over hers, his hands moved lightly, slowly down her body, as if he was trying to memorize every inch and contour. Mariah sighed as she felt his hand on the curve of her back, her derriere, the soft flesh between her thighs and *there*. Everett was stroking her in the place that ached for his touch.

His tongue made love to her mouth, eagerly joining with hers on a wondrous journey of exploration and discovery. Meanwhile, the tips of his fingers danced between the curls as they opened her up like a bud. They caressed and probed her moist entrance before he smoothly slid his finger inside.

"Everett!" she cried, when a second finger joined the first. He circled her sensitive nub with his fingers and she arched against him, wanting more.

He gave her more by deepening his kiss while his fingers went farther, deeper, filling her completely. Mariah arched against him, her muscled walls clasping around him like a vise, but Everett didn't stop. He continued to thrust his fingers inside her. Harder, faster.

Pleasure coursed through Mariah and she could feel her body begin to quake, could hear a loud roaring in her ears just as her orgasm tore through her and she saw stars. She cried out at the release. But before she could recover, Everett left her mouth. She wanted more of his feverish kisses, but instead he placed his mouth where his fingers had been.

He cupped her from behind and brought her even closer, and then his tongue darted inside her.

"Ohmigod!" Mariah swore as she arched off the bed, but Everett grasped both her wrists firmly and had his way with her, tasting every inch of her until a second orgasm hit her and she screamed again.

She was so disoriented, she didn't realize Everett had once more switched positions and was lightly brushing damp tendrils of hair away from her face. "Are you okay?" he asked, looking down at her.

Mariah nodded, but was unable to speak. The kaleidoscope of emotions he'd unleashed was like nothing she'd ever encountered before, and they hadn't yet fully consummated their relationship. She wasn't sure just how much more pleasure she could take. "I… That was incredible," she finally gasped.

"I enjoyed tasting you," Everett said, licking his lips. "I've been craving you for a long time, Mariah."

She smiled weakly. "Have you?"

"Oh, yes." He grinned wickedly. "Which is why I'm giving you time to regain some strength."

"Oh, really? Why is that?"

Everett chuckled. "Oh, baby, that was only the appetizer. We have the main event, dessert, and then there's always seconds."

She titled her head and looked up at him through glazed eyes. "There's more?"

"Oh, much more," Everett murmured, reaching for her. He kissed her openmouthed, absorbing her gasp of surprise, which allowed his tongue to dive inside and explore every inch of her mouth. Sexual hunger emanated from him as he claimed her and made her his.

The feel of Mariah electrified every fiber in Everett's being. He'd been waiting for weeks and, deep down, maybe longer for a woman who could make him feel alive again.

And he had. He'd found that woman in Mariah and he couldn't wait to bury himself inside her. And she was ready for him. He'd ensured that she was wet and primed. And now, reaching for a foil packet from his pants pocket, he protected them both. Once he was sheathed, a fierce rush of sexual need enveloped him, and as if she sensed what he needed, she parted her legs for him and he settled himself between her thighs.

He kissed her wildly, passionately, as he drove his shaft inside her. Mariah groaned as he inched deeper and deeper, filling her completely. Then he began moving slowly, rhythmically. He wanted her to feel each and every stroke, wanted her to know how much he craved her, desired her. And that he was starting to fall in love with her.

Love? His mind wanted to rest on the thought, but the lower half of his body wanted release. He had no choice but to go with it. Back and forth. In and out. Slow and easy, then deeper and deeper.

Mariah's moans became louder as he rocked into her, joining their bodies as one. Her arms circled his neck, pulling his mouth down on hers. There was nothing gentle or tentative about her kiss, either. All the pent-up frustration from weeks of holding back was unleashed and their tongues dueled, wanting mastery. And when Mariah wrapped her legs around his waist, pulling him deeper and deeper inside her tight core, he began pumping harder and faster.

"Yes, oh, yes," she cried, as her release came, simultaneously shattering his control, and his entire body detonated into a million pieces.

Chapter 14

A wet tongue.

Warm hands working their way up and down his pulsing shaft.

Arousal.

Everett felt his body come to life and was momentarily disoriented as sleep began to leave his eyes. He glanced down and saw Mariah, naked on her knees on the bed, with her breasts bobbing forward. He wanted to reach for them, squeeze them and taste them, as he'd done last night.

But instead he was held captive. She was firmly holding him between her hands. He watched as she licked her lips to moisten them, just before taking his rock-hard erection between those full, deliciously sinful lips of hers.

"Sweet Jesus…!" His hips lifted off the bed.

She teased him, taking him deep into the heat of her mouth before releasing him so she could lick, suck, taste him, as he'd done to her last night. Hell, twice this morning. He hadn't been able to get enough of her taste, her smell. Mariah's unique scent was so hot that he might explode right then and there just thinking about that honeyed interior.

And now she was sucking him off as if her life depended on it. It was too much.

"Baby, baby," Everett said, trying to rise from the bed, "you have to stop now."

Mariah shook her head as her eyes connected with his. "Not until I make you come and taste you." She pushed his chest with such force that he fell back against the pillows and finally gave up the control he was so desperately trying to hold on to.

Instead, he just enjoyed her ministrations. The soft feel of her lips on his shaft, the light flicks of her tongue on its length. When she bobbed down again and took him completely into her mouth, Everett grasped her head and ground into her. Mariah took all of him, milking him until he could feel the tension inside his body steadily building and eventually reaching the peak.

"Mariah!" he groaned, just as he shuddered violently and climaxed.

Mariah took him and all his juices. When she was finished and his trembling began to subside; she looked up at him, licked her lips and smiled. "Now we're even."

Sunshine was beaming in from the deck when Mariah finally awoke a few hours later. For a moment, she had no idea what day or time it was. Thanks to the throbbing in her center, all she remembered was making love to Everett all night and most of the morning, until they'd fallen asleep again.

She smiled naughtily when she thought of the way she'd woken him before sunrise, with his manhood in her mouth.

Mariah had no idea what had come over her. She'd always wanted to do it, but it hadn't been her ex's favorite. He'd never been willing to lose control and give up his power by coming in her mouth.

Everett had. He'd trusted her with the most intimate part of himself, and because of it their love-making last night had been incredibly pleasurable and the most thrilling she'd ever had.

The door to their suite opened and Everett walked in carrying a cardboard tray with foam cups of coffee, and a paper bag. "Good morning, or should I say good afternoon?"

Mariah sat up, allowing the sheet to fall from her bare breasts, and reached for a cup. "Good afternoon and thank you."

"You're welcome." Everett sat beside her on the duvet cover and lightly caressed her cheek. "I enjoyed last night immensely."

"So did I." She took a sip of coffee. It wasn't Myers Coffee Roasters, but it would do in a pinch and covered her nervousness. She'd never woken up next to a man other than her ex-husband and was unsure of the proper etiquette. Was there one after they'd just spent all night making love and discovering each other's bodies?

Everett's expression turned serious and contemplative. "I hope you know that I didn't quite intend on coming on so strong. I'd planned to take you out and—"

Mariah placed her index finger over his mouth. "Don't apologize for being spontaneous. We were both living in the moment, which is clearly not something either of us do in our everyday life. Last night, this morning, couldn't have been more perfect."

That brought a wide grin to his gorgeous face, "About this morning…" He rubbed his chin thoughtfully, as if remembering how brazen she'd been in taking his shaft in her palms and making him come inside her mouth. It had felt not only erotic, but empowering, knowing that she could please Everett. "I didn't expect to wake up…"

"With you in my mouth?" she offered devilishly.

For once Everett was the one blushing, and his smile broadened. "Yeah."

"You're always the one giving," Mariah responded. "This morning was for you, about you."

"Has anyone ever told you you're incredible?"

"Not lately."

Everett plucked the coffee cup out of her hand and placed it on the nightstand. "Well, then, allow me to enlighten you." He slid the covers away and lowered her to the pillow.

By early evening, they were back in Seattle after a short ride on the ferry from Bainbridge Island. They were on their way to Everett's parents's place to pick up EJ. Everett hadn't turned toward her apartment, but was heading to his folks' home.

"I'm not properly dressed to meet your parents, Everett." She squirmed beside him in the passenger seat.

"Hogwash, you look spectacular." He eyed her in the tight white jeans, green turtleneck, scarf, denim jacket and riding boots.

"I'm severely underdressed to meet your family."

He patted her thigh. "You'll be fine. They'll love you." *As I do,* he almost added, but refrained. He couldn't give too much of his feelings away before Mariah was ready to hear them.

They pulled up to a wrought-iron black fence with a keypad. After he punched in several digits, the gate opened.

"This is where you grew up?"

He could hear the amazement in Mariah's voice. "Not entirely," Everett answered, even though he'd spent most of his teens here. "It's about ten thousand square feet, with five bedrooms and six and a half baths."

She gave him a curious look, but said nothing as he drove up the long, tree-lined path before pulling into the circular driveway of the large brick house set on more than an acre of land. Four pillars in front made it look like a plantation right out of the South.

"We're here," he said, turning off the engine and disembarking.

He was at Mariah's door in a flash and was glad he was, because the front door opened almost immediately. EJ came out and flew into his arms, shouting, "Dad, Dad!" followed closely by his parents.

Everett bent down and scooped him up. "How's my boy?"

"I'm good," EJ said, wrapping his small arms around Everett's neck and giving him a hug. "I missed you." Then he looked behind him. "Did you bring me something?"

Everett glanced behind him as Mariah exited the vehicle. "You know I always do. Babe," he called out to her, "can you get EJ's gift from the backseat?"

"Babe?" his mother said incredulously from the doorway.

Mariah gave him a hesitant smile. "Of course." She opened the back door and produced a puzzle she'd discovered on the island. "What do you think of this, EJ?" She held out the box as Everett placed the boy back on his feet.

"Thanks!" EJ bent down to start opening it.

"You can do that inside," Everett scolded.

"All right." EJ picked up the box and rushed inside, curious to see what they'd brought him. Everett had told her EJ enjoyed puzzles and she hoped he like the gift.

Everett walked over to Mariah and placed his arm around her waist. He could feel her trembling, and he wished she wouldn't worry, because his parents were pussycats. "Mom, Dad, I'd like you to meet Mariah Drayson, my girlfriend."

Mariah glanced up at him in surprise, but didn't correct him.

"It's a pleasure to meet you, Mariah," Stephen Myers said, smiling at her.

"Please come inside," Gwen added. "There's a chill."

They ended up in the European-style living room, where Everett's father had already started a fire. Mariah noted the plastered beam ceilings, limestone floors and high-end light fixtures, while EJ disappeared into the room his grandparents had set up for him for overnight stays.

"Brandy, son?" Stephen inquired, walking to the wet bar in the corner.

"Love one," Everett responded, as he sat on the plush suede sofa.

"I was just having a glass of Bordeaux, if you'd like one, Mariah," his mother offered.

"I'll have the same," Mariah replied, joining Everett on the sofa. Gwen wasted no time pouring a goblet and handing it to her, then sat on the chaise.

"How did you two meet?" Everett's father asked from the bar.

Everett turned to smile at her. "At Mariah's bakery."

"Oh, so you're the young lady my son told me about," his mother commented.

Mariah seemed surprised and turned to him. "You've been talking about me?"

Gwen laughed. "Yes, nothing but good things. So how was your trip?"

"It was wonderful," Everett reached for Mariah's hand. It was cold and a bit clammy, and he wished she would relax. His parents didn't bite. Especially with him by her side. "Bainbridge Island is a hidden treasure."

"Oh, didn't we visit there once, darling?" His mother glanced up at his father, who was returning with two brandies in hand.

Everett accepted one and sipped generously.

"We did," Stephen responded, sitting beside his wife on the chaise. "It's a great spot for lovers."

She coughed dramatically, as she'd just taken a sip of her wine.

"C'mon, Gwen, we're all adults here." His father laughed. "Don't act so surprised. Plus, it's high time the boy brought a woman home after nearly five years of celibacy. It's a breath of fresh air after losing Sara."

Everett rolled his eyes upward as he felt Mariah stiffen beside him on the sofa. He wished his father hadn't brought up his deceased wife. "Well," he said, then finished the rest of his brandy in one gulp, "I think we should grab EJ and head on home." He prodded Mariah to rise from the sofa and she placed her wine goblet on the table beside his glass.

"Everett, that's fine brandy you have there. It was meant to be sipped," his father reprimanded, sitting upright.

And boy, did he know it. Everett could feel the sting of the burning liquid going down like molten fire in his belly. "Sorry, Dad. We have to get EJ home and ready for school tomorrow."

"Oh." His mother frowned. "We'd hoped you'd stay awhile. We'd like to get to know Mariah."

"And you will," Everett said, speaking for Mariah, who'd suddenly gone as quiet as a mouse. He placed his hand on the small of her back. "I promise. We'll arrange for a dinner real soon."

"It was lovely to have met you," his father said, grasping both Mariah's hands.

"You both as well." She finally spoke as Everett led her to the foyer.

"I'm going to get EJ," he said to her. "I'll be right back, okay?" He hadn't liked the turn the conversation had taken and was eager to get back on the road with EJ and Mariah, and away from painful memories.

Mariah watched Everett climb the winding staircase to the second floor. She'd sensed his unease in the living room and his need for a quick getaway.

"I hope we didn't upset you, dear," his mother said from behind her, "when my husband mentioned Everett's wife, Sara."

"Deceased wife," Stephen corrected, from her side.

Mariah spun around. She hadn't heard them enter the foyer.

"No, no, of course not." She feigned a smile even though her stomach was knotting. It wasn't that she was jealous of Everett's dead wife. How could she be when she knew nothing about her? That's the part of him that Everett kept to himself. He hadn't confided in her even after she'd learned they'd shared a child. Did he not think he could talk to her about Sara?

"It's just that Sara was a big part of this family," his mother continued. "Had been for years, and losing her so suddenly, so tra—" her voice broke slightly "—tragically was a big blow to us and to Everett. He was so devastated—"

"Mother…"

The commanding tone coming from behind them

caused them all to turn around. The scowl on Everett's face as he held EJ to his side was unmistakable.

"I'm sorry, Everett," his mother murmured, clearly embarrassed at having been caught discussing a forbidden topic.

Everett's lips pursed together. "It's fine." He turned to his father. "Thanks for watching EJ for me."

"It was no trouble at all." Stephen Myers lowered himself to EJ's height. "We enjoy having our grandson around. Makes us feel young, right, Gwen?" He looked up at his wife, who had unshed tears in her eyes, but she merely nodded in response.

EJ gave his grandfather a hug. "Bye, Grandpa."

"Mariah?" Everett looked in her direction.

Mariah touched his mother's shoulder. "I'll see you again, sometime soon?"

"I would like that," Gwen whispered.

Mariah followed Everett and EJ out into the night. The air was chilly, but that was nothing compared to Everett's somber mood on the ride to her apartment. He was quiet, leaving EJ to chatter nonstop about the days he'd spent with his grandparents. Mariah couldn't understand why Everett was so upset that his mother had shared that part of him with her. They were dating, after all. Gwen probably assumed they'd spoken of Sara. Perhaps if he'd been more open and forthright, Mariah wouldn't be so desperate for the tiniest scrap of information about her from his parents.

Instead of turning off the engine when they reached her apartment, Everett kept it running as he pulled her suitcase out of the trunk and walked her up the stairs. "You don't have to see me to my door." She glanced behind him at EJ. "It's not good to leave your son in the car by himself with the engine running."

Everett nodded. "I'll see you tomorrow?" He asked it

more as a question instead of making a statement. How could he wonder, when they were so much more than business partners now? He brushed a kiss across her forehead.

"Of course," Mariah responded. She watched him turn to leave and couldn't understand what had just happened. They'd shared one of the sexiest, most romantic nights of her life and she couldn't let it end on a sour note.

Mariah dropped her suitcase and ran after Everett, catching him at the curb. She didn't care that EJ was sitting in the car, staring at them. When she reached Everett and he spun around to face her, she circled her arms around his neck and kissed him hard.

She kissed him passionately, using her mouth, her teeth and her tongue, and pressing her body into his groin to remind him of the mind-blowing sex they'd shared. She pulled away slightly to stare into his dark brown eyes and saw the man she'd been with yesterday. And kissed him again. He responded and pulled her even tighter to him.

Several moments later she could feel his erection pressing firmly against her core. Everett was the first to retreat and step backward. "W-what was that?"

Mariah let out a deep, ragged breath. She was just as affected by the kiss as he was. "A reminder of how good we are. We'll talk tomorrow." She blew a kiss at him and spun on her heel and walked away.

Chapter 15

Mariah had never felt so good. After she'd given Everett a kiss that rocked both their worlds, she'd thought she'd have spent the night worrying about why he was finding it so hard to talk to her about his past. Instead, she'd fallen into a deep sleep, probably because she hadn't gotten much sleep the previous evening after they'd made love all night.

She awoke on Monday morning in much better spirits than she'd gone to bed, excited about the day ahead because construction was starting on the café. They'd finally settled on a contractor and Everett had submitted the final drawings for a permit.

Thanks to Everett's connections, the approval process would be fast-tracked. The contractor had received the okay for an early start so they could begin work, and now Mariah was sure she'd see Everett just about every day throughout the project. He'd indicated he would be very hands-on.

So when he walked in later that morning in trousers and a button-down shirt, Mariah's heart began hammering loudly in her chest. She hadn't thought she'd still feel this giddy around him, but she did, just as she had the first time they'd met. Except this time they weren't strangers. They were lovers.

She watched as he donned a hard hat the foreman had given him. He smiled at her from across the room, causing her to tingle all over. She was so *aware* of him. How could she not be after the intimacies they'd shared on the island? She wondered if her brothers could tell. Chase and Jackson were both huddled in the storefront, whispering about something, while she openly ogled Everett while she acted as if she was stocking the display cases. Instead she was watching his every move.

Once he'd finished with the superintendent, Everett walked straight toward her and, right in front of her brothers, pulled her into his arms and kissed her. She heard the hoots and hollers of Chase and Jackson from behind them, but all she could feel was the thud of her own heart and the warmth of Everett's strong arms around her.

When they separated, Mariah smiled up at him. She wiped some of her lipstick off his lips. "Good morning."

He smiled back. "Good morning."

"As much as I know you lovebirds would like another day off, this is a place of business," Chase teased from behind her.

Everett let her go, much to her consternation. "We'll continue this later," he murmured in her ear. "How about dinner at my place with EJ?"

"At your place? Sure."

They set a time and soon he was waving to her brothers and exiting the bakery.

Jackson winked at her as Everett departed. Mariah

couldn't resist blushing, clearly confirming what he already knew: their relationship had blossomed.

Later than night, Mariah drove over to Everett's. Because it was a school night it had made sense for her to go there, so she brought dinner with her since Margaret had called out ill earlier that day. Everett lived in an upscale part of Seattle in one of the high-rises. She had to be buzzed in by security downstairs, then entered an elevator that climbed to the penthouse floor.

"Chinese food!" EJ yelled, and took the bags from her when she arrived. "Thank you, Miss Mariah," he said over his shoulder as he disappeared in what she assumed was the direction of the kitchen.

Mariah stepped inside and glanced around the elegantly decorated apartment. It was strange that this was her first time over. That's when she realized that Everett had been doing all the giving, all the chasing, and this was the first time she'd made the effort to truly get to know him. No wonder he didn't want to share more about his past with her.

"Can I take your coat?" he asked from her side.

Mariah turned around and allowed him to help her out of the denim jacket she wore over a maxi skirt, tank and crocheted sweater. She'd gone home after the bakery and changed before picking up dinner on the way.

"So, welcome," Everett said, as she walked farther into the living room and took in the modern decor, abstract art, flat-screen television and stunning glass dining table with parson chairs.

She turned to face him. "You didn't decorate this place, did you?"

He stared at her for several long moments before he finally answered, "No, I didn't."

Mariah nodded in understanding and quietly walked

toward the French doors to the terrace. She opened them and stepped out to the railing, staring at the dark sky and stars overhead. She didn't know why it hurt that Everett was still in the same apartment he'd shared with his wife, but it did.

She turned when she heard footsteps and accepted the glass of red wine that Everett held out for her as he joined her. She took a sip and swirled it around in her mouth so she could have time to formulate her thoughts, and turned back to face the city lights. "This is good."

"It's a good vintage," Everett said from her side.

"So, how long have you lived here?" Mariah asked. She was ready to hear more about Sara if Everett was ready to share it.

Everett shrugged. "I don't know. Nine years or so."

He felt fidgety and restless, as he had ever since his mother had brought up Sara's death in front of Mariah the night before, making him relive the aftermath of the accident. It was as if he'd time-traveled back to that awful place five years ago when his whole world had turned on its axis and he'd become a widow and a single father all in one breath.

He knew Mariah's leading question meant that she wanted him to open up about his past, about Sara, and he would. It just wasn't easy going back down the dark road, but last night Mariah had shown him that no matter how bad it was, she wasn't running. In fact, she'd run after him when he'd begun to retreat inside himself, and kissed him until he'd remembered that he was in the present. A present that included Mariah, a woman he was falling in love with.

Mariah sipped her wine.

Everett turned to her and leaned his back against the

stone frame of the balcony. "What's on your mind, Mariah? You have something you want to ask me. Questions. Ask them and I'll try my best to answer them honestly."

Mariah noticed that his voice was thick and unsteady. "All right." She faced him. "Are you still in love with Sara?"

His dark eyes never left hers for an instant and he didn't hesitate when he said, "No."

She felt reassured and nodded. "But you don't like to talk about her? About the past?"

His gaze bored into hers. "No, I don't, but I know that when you're in a relationship, sharing your past and what's shaped you is important. I'm willing to do that for you. If you're willing to do the same."

Mariah blinked and focused on his enigmatic face. He was challenging her. If she expected him to reveal all, it would be a give and take. He wasn't going to bare his heart unless she, too, was ready to talk. "All right!"

EJ stepped into the terrace doorway. "Are we going to eat now? I'm starved."

Everett turned to his son. "Of course. Let's go." He held out his hand to Mariah and she took it.

Later, after they'd finished dinner and watched a television show together and put EJ to bed, Mariah started to follow Everett into his bedroom, but stopped short at the door. She had felt more at ease in the living room, especially with a young, impressionable child in the house, but Everett had been afraid that EJ might overhear them talking and didn't want him to get hurt, so she'd acquiesced.

She stood in the doorway for several moments. When he saw that she hadn't moved, Everett came toward her and said, "It's not the same bed. I had it changed." He pulled her into the bedroom.

"Oh, okay." She hated that he understood part of her unease and insecurity. He began removing his shirt and unbuckling his pants. So she did the same, easing her sweater and tank over her head and sliding her maxi skirt down her legs. When she spun around in her bra and panties, she found Everett's hungry gaze on her. "C-can I have a T-shirt?"

He blinked several times and asked, "What was that?"

"A T-shirt?"

"Oh, yeah, I'll get one for you." He stepped toward another door that Mariah could see led to a large walk-in closet. He returned a few seconds later with a T-shirt in hand and held it out to her.

He didn't turn away as she undressed, and instead watched her unlatch her bra and place it next to her clothes, which she'd folded across a nearby chair, before slipping the T-shirt over her head. "I like you in my shirt," he murmured, throwing the covers back so they could get in.

"And I like wearing it."

He grinned as he pushed the pillows up against the headboard, turned on the lamp on the nightstand and slid into bed. Once he was settled, he held his arms out to her and Mariah slipped under the warm covers and into his embrace. They sat there in silence for what seemed like an eternity before Everett spoke. She was in no rush. She wanted him to talk when he felt ready, and she would listen and be patient, the same way he'd treated her from the beginning.

"Sara and I grew up together," he began. "Our families had known each other for years, but we just saw one another as friends. Until we were older. And one night, after we both had broken up with our respective partners, we were sharing our woes over a bottle of wine and one thing led to another. Sara was worried that it would hurt our friendship, but it didn't, it only added to it. And so, after a year of courtship, we married. A year later, she was pregnant with EJ and we were over the moon."

Everett let out a long sigh and Mariah curled her arms tighter around him, letting him know that it was okay. She was there for him.

"The day EJ was born was one of the single greatest moments of my life." Everett's voice was shaky. "I loved our son and Sara was so happy. We thought we had an entire lifetime ahead of us with our boy, but three years later, she was taken in a blink of an eye." He snapped his fingers.

Mariah slid her hand into his. "What happened?"

"A drunk driver ran a red light and h-hit her head-on. Sh-she was still alive in the hospital and I raced to get to her."

Mariah sat up and looked at Everett's ravaged face. "And did you make it in time?"

He nodded as tears slid down his sculpted cheeks. "Long enough for her to tell me to take care of our son, to give him all the love sh-she wouldn't be able to. I—"

Mariah gulped hard and shook her head as tears welled in her own eyes at seeing her man in so much pain. "You don't have to tell me any more." She couldn't bear to watch him to relive the worst moment of his life.

"I have to," Everett murmured, "because you—you have to know what else she told me."

"What did she say?" Mariah wiped away his tears with the palm of her hand, and then her own.

"She told me not to be afraid to love again and that she was giving me her blessing. Can you believe that?" He cried openly, weeping aloud. "Even when she lay there dying…Sara was thinking of me and telling me that she was giving me permission to love again."

"That was incredibly selfless," Mariah said. "Sounds like she was an amazing woman."

* * *

Everett swallowed hard and bit back more tears. He didn't like what Mariah had just said. "She was, but so are you, babe." He turned slightly so he was facing her and could look into her beautiful brown eyes. "I don't want you comparing yourself to Sara. Because there's no comparison. You're your own woman and I want you for you." He wanted to say more, but didn't, because when he said he loved her, he wanted her to believe it, and not think he was placating her.

"You mean that?" she asked.

"I do." He leaned forward and kissed her forehead, her eyelid, her nose, her cheek before finally brushing his lips across hers. "I do." He wanted Mariah to know he was genuine.

He reached under the covers for the edge of her T-shirt and lifted it over her head. Then he bent down and began kissing his way to her breasts. He looked up at her again and repeated, "I do." Then he took her nipple in his mouth and suckled, while he palmed her other breast, alternating between firm and gentle squeezes.

Mariah began moaning as he laved the turgid bud with the tip of his tongue, before taking it fully into his mouth and sucking hard. "Yes, Everett, like that." Her head fell back on the pillows.

Everett didn't stop there. He made his way from her breasts to plant tender kisses along her abdomen, stomach and the curve of her hips. He scooted farther down the bed and when he reached the waistband of her bikini panties, grasped hold and slid them down her legs. Mariah lifted her feet so he could toss them aside. And that's when he took over, spreading her legs wide, so his eyes could laser focus on the patch of curls between her thighs.

"Look at me, Mariah."

She opened her eyes and stared at him.

"I want you for you," he said, and then darted his tongue inside her moist heat. He took his sweet time going for the prize. Teasing her until she whimpered in protest. He lifted his head. "And I want you to come for me. Come for me."

"Yes, for you," she cried.

Like a missile heading toward its target, his tongue went straight to her clitoris and when he reached the nub, his tongue ran over it with gentle sweeps at first. And then he sucked, causing Mariah to cry out as her thighs began to quiver uncontrollably. Everett felt the power of her orgasm hit her, but he didn't stop, just kept sucking until she fell backward on the bed. Only then did he raise his head, remove his boxers and glide atop her body. But instead of stopping their lovemaking, he lifted her legs over his shoulders and slid inside her wet heat. He felt as if he was home when Mariah welcomed him, her body stretching so he could fill her completely.

Everett grasped both sides of her face and plunged his tongue inside her mouth while his erection thrust deep inside her. He could see she was loving the angle because she undulated against him, and Everett was lost in the sweet sensation of being inside her, having her muscled walls contracting all around him. It didn't take long for him to come with a roar, his own release triggering another contraction from Mariah as ripple after ripple of pure pleasure soared through them.

"Everett," Mariah said a while later, after they'd both recovered from the mind-blowing sex. "It's never been this way for me before."

"You mean our lovemaking?" he asked, peering at her, where she was lying on his chest.

She nodded. "In my marriage, it wasn't this enjoyable."

"You have no idea what this is doing for my ego," he said, smiling down at her.

"It was just routine," Mariah admitted, glancing up from under hooded lashes. "But with you, it's intense and passionate and I can't count how many orgasms I've had while we've been together." Since he'd been so open and honest, Mariah wanted to share more with him, be more open herself.

"I'm glad you shared that with me."

She wished she could reveal more, such as her struggles with getting pregnant during her marriage. Or that one of the reasons sex had become so routine and boring was because of her infertility issues. But her relationship with Everett was still so new, so young. She didn't want to introduce this kind of drama, at least not yet. She just wanted to be with him and enjoy the moment. But in the back of her mind, Mariah knew it was just a matter of time time before her past came back to haunt her.

Chapter 16

"Belinda, it's so good to hear from you," Mariah said several nights later, while she munched on some popcorn at her apartment. She was on her own tonight because Everett had a parent-teacher meeting for EJ. They'd been spending almost every night together since their return from Bainbridge Island.

Mariah hadn't minded, because she needed some time to assess everything that had happened between them in the last week. She and Everett had gone from two people attracted to each other to lovers all in the span of a month. She hadn't moved this fast in her prior relationship with her ex-husband. They'd taken things much slower, but look where they'd ended up! The extra time had meant nothing because they'd still broken up.

While her relationship with Everett was progressing quickly, the chemistry between them was palpable and all-consuming. They'd moved well beyond the physical when he'd opened up to her about losing his wife. Mariah had watched him struggle with his emotions, and though he'd been open and upfront with her, she hadn't done the same and she felt guilty. She'd wanted to tell him all, but was scared of how he might react.

"Well, I figured I had to check on you," Belinda responded from the other end of the line, "because you've been MIA for weeks. Last I heard, you were opening a Myers Coffee Roasters in the bakery. So imagine my surprise when I hear from Grandma that you've created a new pastry sensation and didn't even share it with me."

Mariah sighed. "I'm so sorry, Belinda, it's just been crazy around here. Everything is happening so fast."

"Is that because of a certain owner of Myers Coffee Roasters? I know he was coming on pretty strong."

Mariah chuckled. "You know it is." She smiled, thinking of her man.

"So dish," Belinda exclaimed. "Catch me up on everything I've missed."

Mariah filled her in on how well the construction of the Myers Coffee Roasters' on-site café at the bakery was going. She told her cousin how Everett made his presence known not just for the café, but because of his personal interest in Mariah.

"So eventually I gave in and agreed to a date," Mariah continued, "because he wasn't going to give up."

"He's a smart man," Belinda replied. "You just needed to be courted."

Mariah laughed. "Something like that. And our relationship has blossomed from there and..." She paused for several beats. "Last weekend, we went away together."

Belinda giggled like a schoolgirl. "Oh, and how was that?"

"Scary, exciting, thrilling," Mariah answered. "It was

more than I could have ever imagined. And between us girls, better than any sex Rich and I ever had."

"Well then!" Mariah heard Belinda snap her fingers. "So what's next?"

Mariah hunched her shoulders as if her cousin could see her. "I don't know. Everything is going great. I've met his parents and and his son, and he's opened up to me about his deceased wife, but…"

"But what?"

"He doesn't know."

"That you might not be able to have kids?" Belinda offered.

"Yes," Mariah said, as a solitary tear trickled down her face. She wiped it away with the back of her hand. "What if he wants more kids? What do I do then?"

"Have you guys talked about children?"

"No, but—"

Belinda interrupted her. "No buts. Don't look at the cart before the horse. If he hasn't said anything, there's no reason for you to get upset about a phantom baby."

Mariah tried taking a deep breath, but it didn't work. "You say that now, but Everett is a good man and a wonderful father. I can't see him not wanting to expand his family."

"When the time comes, you guys will talk about it calmly and rationally. You'll share with him your struggles, and if he's the man you think he is, the man I suspect you're falling for, he won't care."

"I hope you're right," Mariah said.

"I am," Belinda stated emphatically. "You'll see."

As she hung up with her cousin, Mariah certainly hoped she was right, because Belinda was correct about one thing. Mariah was starting to fall hard for Everett and it would break her heart if he turned his back on her. But wasn't it inevitable, when she was less than a woman?

Mariah stared at the café. They were three weeks into construction and already had framing and rough-ins for the ceiling, electrical and mechanical completed and had received their building inspections. Drywall was now being hung and taped so the seams wouldn't be visible.

It was really starting to come together and in a couple more weeks they would be open. Mariah moved away from the storefront. Mariah was heading toward the kitchen to bring out more pastries when to her surprise her father walked in.

"Daddy!" Mariah rushed toward him, enveloping him in a hug. "What are you doing here?"

"Well, I thought I'd see how business was coming along." He glanced at the plywood door covering the café's entrance. "What's going on here?"

"Remember, I told you about it a few weeks ago?" she said. "We're partnering with Myers Coffee Roasters and we'll have a café on-site. Isn't that great?"

"You got Everett Myers to contribute to this place?"

"Don't sound so shocked," Mariah replied with a frown. Was it entirely out of the realm of possibility that Everett could see potential in Lillian's?

"It's not that, baby girl. I just don't want you to fail and get in over your heads," her father said.

Mariah folded her arms across her chest. "So Mother's been whispering in your ear."

"Oh, now, don't go harping on your mother. She and I only want what's best for you, for all of you."

"I know, but we have it under control. How about I show you around?" She linked her arm through one of his.

When they entered the kitchen, Jackson was just as surprised as she was to see their father. "Pops!" He greeted him warmly with a handshake.

Graham looked around the kitchen with its gleaming ovens, stoves and mixing equipment. "It's quite an impressive operation you've got going on here."

"We try," Jackson said with a sly grin. "Would you like something?" He gestured toward the chocolate chip cookies that he'd just taken out of the oven and were cooling on the racks.

"Oh, I don't know." Their father rubbed his stomach. "You know your mother doesn't like me eating sweets."

"It can't hurt this once." Jackson reached over and grabbed a cookie. "Try one."

Sure enough, Graham Drayson couldn't resist a hot chocolate chip cookie and devoured it within seconds. When he was done, he wiped his mouth with the paper towel Mariah supplied him with. "So when does the café open?" He pointed toward the storefront.

"In a couple of weeks," Mariah responded. "I would love it if you could attend the grand opening."

He kissed her forehead. "Of course, sweetheart.

Mariah sighed inwardly. She didn't know why she thought he might come without her, as he'd done today. She offered a weak smile. "Great!"

"Jackson, come here." Their father motioned him forward and pulled them both into a semicircle.

"Can anyone get on this action?" Chase asked, leaning in the doorway. He must have heard all the ruckus from the office. He stood there sans glasses, watching them.

"C'mon, son." Their father pulled Chase over into their tight unit. "Although I may not always agree with your choices, I want you to know that I love all three of you and will always be here for you, no matter what. Believe that."

"We do," Mariah said. "But it's always good to hear."

* * *

Everett stopped by her apartment for dinner the following evening, since EJ was at a friend's for a sleepover. It was the first time Mariah had allowed Everett or any man other than her brothers into her home. Initially, it had been hard getting used to having her own place, because once she'd she left her parents she'd gone to college, and then moved in with Rich as his wife. So essentially she'd never truly been on her own before, and it had been disconcerting. When they'd divorced, it had been an adjustment coming home every night to an empty apartment. The loneliness had been a silent reproach about all that had gone wrong in her marriage.

But having Everett here in her place was such a natural progression of their relationship. She was grateful that he'd opened up to her about Sara, and Mariah wanted to do the same and be as transparent as he'd been.

As a thank-you, she'd decided to make him a home-cooked meal of beef Wellington with salad, and a chocolate soufflé that she'd mastered during her lonely afternoons in her marriage.

Ever the gentleman, Everett arrived holding a bottle of wine, as well as a bouquet of roses. He was dressed in denims and a black T-shirt. She wasn't used to seeing him so casual, but it looked damn good on him. As for the flowers, she put them in a vase and led him to the kitchen, where she was preparing dinner. She filled him in on her father's unexpected visit.

"So your dad stopped by the bakery, unannounced?"

"Yes, he did," Mariah replied, refocusing her energies on cutting vegetables for the salad. "I was surprised, considering he and Mother have been dead set against our business venture. But I think he was curious, and at least that's more than Mother's done."

Everett must have detected the note of hostility in her voice because he said, "You and your mom truly don't get along."

Mariah shrugged. "Wish I knew why. Because I have always tried to be the perfect daughter. I tried to be the epitome of grace and class. I never dressed like the other girls in school because image was everything to my mother. In the end, I failed."

"You're talking about your divorce?"

"I was a disgrace," Mariah said, remembering the horrible argument they'd had when she'd informed Nadia that her marriage was over. "There hasn't been a divorce in the Drayson family in years. What had I done to cause him to walk away, she'd demanded to know, because of course, it had to have been me." Mariah furiously cut the cucumbers on the chopping block. "The fault couldn't be with Rich. He could never be lacking as a husband."

Everett walked over to her, took the knife out of her hand and placed it on the counter. He grasped her by the shoulders, forcing her to look at him. "It wasn't your fault alone. There were two people in the marriage."

"I know. I just spent much of my life trying to make Mom happy and failing miserably." Mariah sniffed.

"Parents can be hard to please," Everett commented. "Which is why I stopped trying long ago. Now I think my parents and I have come to an understanding. They know I'll always listen to their advice, but may not heed it. The thing is, I'm happy with myself either way. In time, you'll get there, too, and be happy with who you are."

"It's hard to teach an old dog new tricks, right?" Mariah laughed bitterly. "C'mon, help me set the table."

An hour later, after they'd eaten the delicious dinner, they brought their soufflé ramekins to the sofa to watch television. Mariah was wrapped up in Everett's arms when he asked out of the blue, "You've alluded to your marriage quite a bit, but not really told me much about its demise."

Mariah had been dreading this moment, when Everett would want to know more. She would share with him as much as she was able to. "Rich and I met in college and our relationship was fun and carefree. He proposed right after we graduated and it seemed like the next logical step. But the thing is, we hadn't really talked about the future and what we really wanted out of life. Or what were deal breakers."

"Something happened?"

Mariah nodded, sorting through her mind what she could share without getting into the baby-making fiasco. "We were too young, not ready for real life and the struggles that come with it. And when things got tough, Rich got going."

"So you didn't want the divorce?"

Mariah looked at Everett and could see the question in his eyes. "I'm not still in love with him, if that's what you're asking. Our marriage was over long before we signed the divorce papers. It was just that, like my mother, I thought that marriage was for life. We made vows. So I was prepared to dig in the trenches and try to weather the tough times."

"But your ex didn't want to?"

She pointed her index finger. "Precisely. And as you've stated, it takes two. Ultimately, we wanted different things, and instead of growing together and becoming stronger after the tough times, we grew apart."

Mariah wanted to say more, but couldn't. She'd already shared one of her worst failures in life, but to tell him about their infertility problems, too? If she opened Pandora's box and let those old wounds out, she might never get them back in and they'd pull her under. Pull their relationship under.

Mariah didn't want that. She wanted a clean slate with Everett, without all the baggage of her past weighing them down. But was she deluding herself? Could their relationship really survive without full disclosure?

"You okay?" Everett hugged her tighter.

"As long as I have you?" Mariah asked. "I am."

And she meant it. She'd tried hard not fall in love with Everett Myers, but it was impossible not to. He was everything she'd been waiting her whole life to find: an honest, caring, compassionate man who loved his family, was a great father, a respected and fair businessman and a philanthropist all rolled into one. She couldn't be luckier to have found him. And now that she had, she would fight tooth and nail to keep her man.

Chapter 17

Everett didn't see Mariah much over the next two weeks except for the odd time or two when they squeezed in a night together. She was either too tired from the bakery or he was too busy with work or EJ, but he eventually made a quick visit to check on the progress of the café, to ensure they would be ready to open the following Monday.

She quickly grabbed his hand and opened the plywood door. Once inside, Everett was shocked by what he saw. The café was darn near built. The walls were up and painted, the millwork and countertop installed and the Myers Coffee Roasters sign hung down from the rafters.

He'd kept up with Mariah via phone and knew they were much further along than the schedule the contractor had provided, because he'd been promised a bonus if he finished earlier than expected. Everett could see he intended to claim that bonus.

Mariah gazed at him, her eyes large and welcoming. "Well?" She swept her arm around. "What do you think?"

Everett glanced at his surroundings. "This is fantastic, Mariah," he said, grabbing her in his arms and spinning her. "I had no idea." He was truly speechless, which was rare for him.

She nodded. "I know, right? Your vision really came together."

"Yeah, but I had no idea we were this far along."

"They've been moving pretty quickly," Mariah said. "I think we'll be ready to open after final inspections, cleanup, and of course, you need to stock the café on your end with the supplies and equipment."

"I'm ready," Everett said, peering down into her warm eyes. "The equipment was ordered and is sitting in my warehouse, ready for delivery."

"That's great." Mariah beamed. "Do you think you could be ready to open next week? I can't wait for my customers to try the Draynut."

He knew she was excited not only for the café but to debut her new creation. "Absolutely, we'll be ready. And once the customers taste your Draynut and my coffee, we'll be a surefire hit."

"Sounds good to me. How about a kiss before you leave?"

He had no problem complying with that request. He bent to kiss her, long and slow, and the world righted around him at last. He couldn't let days go by without kissing her, feeling her soft curves against him. "I missed this," he murmured, "missed you." In a short span of time, Mariah had become a big part of his life. He'd thought it would scare him, feeling this way again after the way he'd lost Sara, but it didn't. He welcomed it because it meant he was finally moving on with his life.

"We'll see each other on Friday," Mariah reminded him.

"I know, but it's so far away." He pulled her closer so she could feel his arousal pulsating between them. It didn't take much when he was around Mariah to get him aroused. She had that effect on him.

"Keep it in your pants," she said with a chuckle. "I promise to work off all that frustration *on Friday.*"

Slowly, Everett released her. "Promises, promises. I hope you're ready to keep them."

She smiled wickedly at him as she licked her lips. "Oh, I am. You'll see."

Mariah was excited about her plans with Everett. Although it was a weekday, having Kelsey help Jackson and Nancy in the bakery, Mariah was able to take Friday off. It had worked out perfectly with EJ's schedule, because he was home from school for a teachers' prep day. Mariah would finally get the chance to spend more time getting to know him. Everett's son was the most important person in his life and she wanted EJ to like her. It seemed he did, if their first lunch and subsequent dinner at the penthouse was any indication. And today, they'd be spending the whole day together at the Northwest Trek Wildlife Park.

EJ had wanted to do something fun and Mariah had heard about the park, which allowed visitors to see animals up close and have a zip line excursion. Although she was scared to death of heights, she knew that an eight-year-old boy like EJ would love it. After she'd confirmed the zip-lining was for five-year-olds and up, Everett had been on board.

And now they were in his Escalade on their way to the wildlife park. EJ oohed and ahhed when he saw the foothills of Mount Rainier. He talked animatedly during the entire hour-long drive south of Seattle.

"Are you excited?" Mariah asked him after they'd disembarked from the vehicle. Everett pulled out the backpack she'd stocked with bottled water and light snacks.

"I'm totally stoked," EJ said, grinning from ear to ear. "I can't wait to zip-line."

"How do you feel about that?" Everett asked Mariah as he closed the trunk and slid the backpack on.

"Oh, I don't know," she answered honestly.

"Are you scared, Miss Mariah?" EJ inquired. "If I can do it, you can." And off he went, running toward the ticket booth.

Famous last words, thought Mariah.

After they'd received their tickets, they boarded a tram for a narrated fifty-minute drive thorough the park's 435-acre free-roaming area for the animals. They saw different kinds, from bison to moose to caribou herds.

"What's that over there?" EJ asked when they passed a large animal with antlers.

"That's an elk," Everett answered.

"And what's that?" EJ pointed to another animal with antlers that curved under. He was so curious he asked questions constantly.

"That's a bighorn sheep," the guide responded.

EJ snapped pictures with the camera Everett had loaned him. "This is awesome, Dad," he said, turning to his father and Mariah, who were sitting behind him on the tram.

"I'm glad you like it," Everett replied. "But this was Miss Mariah's idea." He gave her a wink.

"I aim to please," she said with a smile.

They continued touring the wooded exhibits to see the bear habitats, then stopped for lunch before heading to the wetlands to see river otters and beavers play in the water. Mariah was enjoying the experience more because she was seeing through a child's eyes, EJ's eyes, and it made it all the more exciting.

Eventually they made their way to the zip line complex. Mariah glanced around at the aerial course. "Looks pretty challenging," she commented. She was rooted to the spot and watching other climbers above her.

"Don't be a chicken," Everett said, tickling her side. "Let's do this." He pulled her toward the entrance.

The guides suited the three of them up in helmets, as well as safety gear around their thighs and waists. EJ was so excited he was talking a mile minute. Meanwhile Mariah's heart thumped loudly in her chest.

"Listen to me," Everett said, pulling her to a stop and grabbing both sides of her helmet. "You're going to be fine. You're not by yourself. I'm here with you and we're doing this together, okay?"

Tears formed in her eyes at Everett's kindness and all Mariah could do was nod. A bit later she kicked herself for being afraid, once she found how fun the discovery and aerial courses were. Most required them to be agile, balanced and mentally tough to get across the tightrope and swinging logs, but Mariah did it. EJ, on the other hand, was a little monkey and easily maneuvered over the climbing wall and obstacle course with grace and nimbleness, much like his father did.

"That was awesome!" the boy said as they made their way toward the exit after they'd finished the zip line adventure. They'd been at the park nearly the entire day. "We have to do that again. Can we, Dad?"

"Sure can," Everett said, laughing at his son.

"And you'll come, too, Miss Mariah?" EJ asked, turning around to face her.

Mariah's heart soared that EJ would want her to come with them. She glanced over at Everett when she said, "Absolutely."

* * *

On the drive ride back to Seattle, the car was quiet, because EJ had promptly fallen asleep after all the day's activities, while Mariah was introspective. Everett reached for her hand as the sun had set during the drive. "Everything all right?" he asked, hazarding a glance in her direction.

"Yeah, I'm good."

"You sure?" He wondered what was on her mind. He hoped EJ hadn't been too much to handle today. Everett was used to his hyperactive son, but this was the first time Mariah had spent the entire day with them and he hoped she wasn't spooked.

She turned and smiled at him. "Today was pretty incredible."

Everett's heart swelled in his chest and he let out a deep sigh. "It was, wasn't it?"

She nodded and he was surprised when he saw unshed tears in her eyes. "EJ's a wonderful little boy," she declared.

"Thank you." He reached across and stroked her cheek. "And you're wonderful, too. Not many women would be game to zip-line through the air like you did. You continue to surprise me, Mariah Drayson."

Once they reached his penthouse, Everett carried EJ inside, while Mariah followed with the backpack. She was removing the remnants in the kitchen when Everett came up behind her at the sink and wrapped his big strong arms around her waist. "EJ's knocked out."

"Oh, yeah."

"So it's just the two of us," he said, seconds before his mouth nuzzled her neck. That left his hands free to roam over her body. When he found her breasts, he molded them in his palms. He loved the feel of them, soft and pliant.

Mariah let out a low purr. "Mmm…"

"You like that?" he whispered, taking the tip of her ear in his mouth and sucking.

"Oh, yes." Her head fell back against his shoulder as he continued tonguing her ear. His hands moved to the waistband on her jeans and pulled her shirt free, before he slipped his fingers inside. He pushed past the waistband of her panties and slid his hand lower. When he reached those damp curls, he groaned and then delved his fingers inside her core.

"Ah…" Mariah let out a deep sigh as he began stroking her.

"I've been wanting to do this all day," Everett murmured as his tongue darted in and out of her ear, mimicking what his fingers were doing inside her womanhood. Mariah began to undulate her buttocks against the hardness in his jeans. "That's right, love. I want you to come for me," he told her.

"Wh-what if EJ wakes up?" Mariah whispered, glancing in the direction of the hallway. She wouldn't want him to walk in on them in flagrante, especially since he was still getting to know her.

"Don't worry about my son, he's a hard sleeper," Everett said as his fingers quickened and he began thrusting deeper inside her. "So you can come as loud as you want."

"I—I can't!"

"Yes, you can." He squeezed one of her nipples through her shirt and twirled it between his thumb and index finger. "Come for me now."

"I—"

Everett wasn't taking no for answer; he wanted her to let go. He grabbed hold of one of her thighs, lifting it to give him better access so he could surge deeper, farther.

"Now!" He groaned into her ear as he teased her clitoris with quick flutters of his thumb.

Mariah compiled and her entire body quaked around his fingers. Her head fell back against him as an orgasm overtook her. When the last of the trembles subsided, Everett removed his hands from her jeans and spun her around to face him. He grasped both sides of her face and kissed her deeply, then bent and lifted her off her feet. Mariah wrapped her legs around his waist as he carried her from the kitchen to his bedroom.

When they arrived, Everett kicked the door shut with his boot and headed straight for the bed. He lowered Mariah to the mattress, but didn't release her mouth. She surrendered to his kiss and the torrent of sensations that exploded inside her as he nipped and sucked.

Eventually, he left her lips so he could bury his face in her neck and lick his way from her collarbone to her ear. Then he rose on his knees so he could start stripping. She was as hungry as he was, judging by how their clothes went flying every which way until they were both naked on the bed. He flipped her over onto her stomach and his firm, erect penis found its way to her wet passage.

He thrust inside her in one fluid movement and then began moving. He wanted her so badly and didn't understand why the need to possess her was so strong, but it was as if they were the only two people on earth and all that existed was the two of them and this moment.

Mariah didn't shy away from the intensity of his lovemaking. In fact, she seemed to welcome it, especially when he put his hands under her and lifted her so her curvy derriere could meet his thrusts, while the other hand fingered her clitoris.

She moaned, telling him she was enjoying everything he was doing. "Yes, Everett, like that." Her cries split the air and she repeated his name when her orgasm tore through her. "Everett, Everett, Everett."

He didn't hear her, couldn't, because he was lost in sensation, grinding his hips into her backside until the heat between them hit a fever pitch. And before he knew it, nirvana struck and his body jerked as the full force of his climax hit him. "God, I love you," he groaned in her ear, holding Mariah close as he collapsed on top of her.

In the aftermath, as they both lay sated on his bed, Everett realized exactly what he'd just said. He'd admitted that he loved Mariah. Had she heard him, since she, too, had been in the midst of euphoria? Although he'd intended to keep his feelings inside, he'd meant those words. He was in love with Mariah. Could she feel the same way?

Chapter 18

Mariah was awake even though her eyes remained closed. How could she sleep after what Everett had just said? He'd told her he loved her. Had it been in the heat of the moment? This wouldn't be the first time it had happened. Friends had told her that men could say things during the heat of passion that they didn't intend to. Had Everett meant it? Or did he wish he could take it back?

She was feigning sleep now because she wasn't sure what to do. She so desperately wanted to say it back to him, but she needed to hear it again to be sure that he'd meant it and hadn't just been overcome with emotion.

Mariah felt Everett stroking her hair as she lay against his chest, her favorite position when they slept together. "Mariah, are you awake?"

"Hmm...?" She rubbed her eyes and then glanced at him.

His own eyes were fathomless and she couldn't read what he was thinking, what he was feeling, until he said quickly, "I meant what I said."

"What?"

"Don't play coy, Mariah. I know you heard me," he replied. His dark gaze bored into hers, challenging her to lie and say otherwise.

She scooted upward toward the pillow so she could face him at eye level. Her eyes fluttered closed and then she opened them to look back up at him. "Yes, I heard you."

Everett reached across the short distance between them and pulled her closer until they were a breath apart. "I love you, Mariah."

Her voice caught in her throat. He'd repeated it, so he must mean it. She was about to repeat the words when Everett continued speaking.

"I know it may seem fast, but I can see a life with you, Mariah. Me, you and EJ, and maybe adding a little brother or sister one day."

All the air in the room suddenly seemed to evaporate for Mariah. She'd been dreading this moment. The day when Everett would say something that would ruin all chances of there ever being a future between them. And it had come. Just as she'd predicted it would. Except there wasn't an easy way for her to extricate herself from the situation without maximum damage.

The man she loved, who'd just said that he loved her back, wanted children, more children *with her*, which she knew was impossible or damn near. She'd tried unsuccessfully for nearly three years to get pregnant with Rich's child and couldn't. It had destroyed their marriage. She couldn't do it again. She couldn't, wouldn't put herself or Everett through that kind of pain, heartbreak and continued disappointment, month after month, year after year. He deserved more. He deserved a woman who could give him babies, lots of babies. He didn't deserve someone who was damaged goods.

"I—I have to go," Mariah said abruptly, and threw the covers back. In the darkness, she searched for her clothes, which they'd discarded in a hurry during the heat of the moment.

"What?" The expression on Everett's face was both hurt and disbelieving.

They'd just made passionate love together as if their lives depended on it, and she was running away. She had no choice. She had to do it now. It was bad enough that she'd allowed their relationship to get this far. She should have known that happiness wasn't in the cards for her, but she'd so desperately needed this and desired him that she hadn't wanted to see they were headed for disaster.

Mariah couldn't speak, couldn't look at him as she found her panties and slipped them up her legs.

"Mariah!" Everett sat upright. "What are you doing?"

"I have to go," she said. "I have an early morning tomorrow and—"

"That's crap and you know it," he responded. "You're running away again. Are you running because I said I love you?" He rose from the bed in all his naked splendor and faced her. "You—you don't have to say it back, not until you're ready. It's just that I…" He paused, as if trying to find the right words. "I was just overcome in the moment."

Mariah didn't dare look up at him as she wrangled with her jeans. If she did, she might give in and he'd drag her back to bed and make love to her again and again, not knowing that there was only the slightest chance that she would ever carry his child. She just couldn't do that to him.

When she didn't speak, his voice turned cold, "Mariah, please say something. And for God's sake, look at me."

Gathering all her inner strength and courage, Mariah took a deep breath and glanced up at Everett. Pain and hurt were etched across his handsome face, a face she loved.

She hated that she was the cause of it and tears sprang to her eyes.

Everett softened immediately and he brushed them away with the pads of his thumbs. "Don't cry, baby. Just come back to bed and talk to me, okay? Whatever it is, we can work through it together."

Mariah shook her head. "I can't. I just can't." She wrenched away from him and, without a glance behind, ran out of the bedroom. She had to. It was for his sake as well as hers.

As she sat in the taxicab that the shocked doormen had so graciously procured for her at this late hour, Mariah pondered what had occurred. She was no good for Everett and he would only resent her in the end, as Rich had. She never wanted to see in Everett's eyes the same look Rich had given her. So if that meant she was destined to be alone, then that was her lot in life and she was just going to have accept it.

Everett stared into his coffee mug as he sat in his office at the Myers Hotel the next morning. He'd gone through the motions of getting dressed and having a big Saturday breakfast with EJ, but his heart wasn't in it. Everett had dropped his son off with his grandparents and made his way to the office, hoping that work would be a distraction. It wasn't. It had been hours and he'd finally hit a wall. He still couldn't believe that after they'd shared an idyllic day together with his son, made love as if they were last two humans on earth and he'd said he loved her, Mariah had walked out on him.

She hadn't given him a reason for her behavior. She'd just stormed out of his bedroom in the middle of the night, for Christ's sake. Everett ran his hand over his head. He couldn't understand it. Should he have waited to tell he loved her? Clearly. But her over-the-top reaction had stunned him. She'd completely shut him out, reverting to the Mariah of old, who had brick walls barricaded around her heart. If he was honest, he was not only hurt; he was angry. Was having his love that abhorrent that she'd had to rush out of his bed?

Everett just couldn't understand and started analyzing those last few moments. That's when it hit him. If he'd read her expression correctly, perhaps it wasn't the idea that he loved her that had freaked her out. She'd become silent when he'd mentioned wanting more kids and giving EJ a little brother or sister. Did her reaction mean that she didn't want kids?

Everett leaned back in his chair. How could that be? Mariah was so great with EJ and clearly adored his son. He could see her as a mother. Had he really been wrong about her? He shook his head.

Darn it! He wanted a big family. Had always wanted one even when he'd been with Sara, but it hadn't been in the cards. But Mariah? He was in love with her and knew she would be a good mother if she could overcome her fears. But what if she wouldn't? Didn't want to? Would he be willing to give up his dream of enlarging his family for Mariah? This whole time he'd been under the assumption that they were on the same page and that she'd be open to starting a family with him. But perhaps they weren't. Was this a deal breaker?

Or had she run away because he'd said he loved her and she wasn't ready yet?

He had to know for sure one way or the other.

Rising from his chair, Everett put on his suit jacket and headed toward the door. After everything they'd shared, he deserved answers from Mariah and he wasn't going to take no for answer until he had them. It shouldn't surprise her, because that had been his MO from the beginning.

Everett made it to Lillian's in half an hour. He swung open the door and searched the storefront for Mariah's honey-blond head.

"Hey, boss," Amber yelled from the café.

Everett glanced up and started toward her. She was stocking shelves with Myers Coffee Roasters. "Amber, have you seen Mariah?"

"Sorry, I haven't," Amber said. "Is there anything I can do?"

He shook his head and without another word to Amber left the café and stalked purposely toward the kitchen. Jackson was coming out with a large silver pan and stopped short when he saw him. "Everett, what's up?" he asked.

"I'm looking for Mariah."

Jackson frowned. "She's not here. Didn't she tell you?"

"Tell me what?" Everett asked impatiently. He needed to find Mariah and talk to her. He didn't have time for riddles.

"Mariah called Chase and me early this morning and told us she wouldn't be in today," Jackson replied. "Said she was going to Chicago for the weekend."

"Chicago!" Everett roared.

Jackson took a step backward. "Hey. Listen, man. Perhaps that temper is the reason my sister rushed off to Chicago in the middle of the night."

Everett dragged in a deep breath, trying to calm his frayed nerves. "I'm sorry for raising my voice, but that's not the reason Mariah left."

"What then?"

"That's between me and your sister," Everett responded. "Should she happen to call you, you can let her know I'm ready to listen when she's ready to talk."

Without another word, he strode from the bakery.

Once he reached his car, Everett slammed his fist on the steering wheel. When was Mariah going to get tired of running and instead fight for what they had? Turning on the ignition, he headed back toward the hotel.

"Not that I'm not excited to see you and all," Belinda said from the driver's side of her sports car as she glanced sideways at her cousin. "But an early morning phone call to come get you at the airport wasn't quite what I expected when I asked you to keep in touch."

Mariah sighed heavily. "Sorry for the short notice, cuz. I just needed to get away in a hurry." She'd called Belinda early that morning after she'd booked a spur-of-the-moment flight from Seattle to Chicago.

Belinda glanced at her again. "Is this about you and Everett?"

Mariah was silent and glanced out the window. She had come to Chicago for a sympathetic ear. Although she and Amber were forging a friendship, it was nice to confide in family.

"How about we talk over pastries at Lillian's?" Belinda inquired. "I bet we can find something there to cheer you up."

"Sounds good." But Mariah didn't look up from the window.

Once they made it to the Magnificent Mile and parked in the garage reserved for Lillian's, they walked the short distance on Michigan Avenue to the store.

When she entered, the familiarity of her surroundings brought a smile to Mariah's face, as did the smell of fresh baked goods. The bakery was similar in design to Lillian's of Seattle, but was bit more ornately decorated than their store due to its prime location on Chicago's most famous street.

"Mariah, is that you?" Shari Drayson said from behind the counter. "What the heck are you doing here?"

"She's here for a weekend retreat," Belinda replied, as Mariah surveyed their storefront displays for a breakfast treat.

"Give me a hug," Shari said, coming around the corner with her arms open wide.

Mariah turned from the display case and saw Shari's pregnant belly bump. Her hand flew to her mouth and she cried, "Omigod!" and rushed toward the back of the bakery.

Shari grabbed her pregnant stomach as she watched Mariah flee past her. She turned to her sister. "Was it something I said?"

Belinda shook her head. "No, it's not you. Let me go talk to her."

Mariah had found her way to the administrative offices in the back of the bakery and shut the door. She sat down in the conference room and cried. She cried for everything she'd never had and never would. Several minutes later, she heard a soft knock on the door. "Come in."

Belinda walked in and closed the door behind her. She headed toward Mariah and offered her a handkerchief. Mariah gratefully accepted and blew her nose. "Thank you."

Her cousin gave her a smile as she sat down beside her. "How you doing?"

Mariah shook her head. "I'm a mess. Shari must think I'm insane. Did you see how she clutched her stomach when I ran by? I must have scared the living daylights out of her."

Belinda chuckled. "More like startled her by your reaction."

"I'll apologize to her."

"You're just one raw nerve, Mariah, if seeing Shari's pregnancy can affect you this way. What's going on?"

Mariah nodded in agreement. "I know I am. And I can tell that I overreacted just now. I guess the timing of seeing Shari, after last night with Everett, was just too much."

"What happened?"

Mariah looked upward and blinked several times. "Everything."

"How about we get those pastries to go and talk at my place?" Belinda suggested.

Mariah gave a weak smile. "Sounds great."

Their talk didn't happen until later that evening, because as soon as they arrived at Belinda and Malik's condominium on Lake Shore Drive, Mariah begged off for a nap. When she awoke, it was dark out. She hadn't meant to sleep the day away, but the strain and exhaustion of the last twenty-four hours had caught up to her. She'd traveled to the wildlife park and back to Seattle after zip-lining, she and Everett had made incredible love, then she'd run back to her apartment.

She'd been unable to sleep and had gotten on her computer to make travel arrangements to Chicago. She'd needed to get away and think. Figure out what she was going to do next. She knew that running out of Everett's apartment had been wrong. She also knew she would have to face him soon, but in that moment she hadn't been able to. And knowing Everett, he wasn't going to accept her leaving him with no explanation and would hunt her down until they hashed things out.

She'd been right. As she looked down at her cell phone, which she'd silenced while she napped, she could see that she'd missed several calls and texts from Everett. The last one from him said Fight for us. She knew he was right. She'd done the exact opposite by running away to Chicago.

There'd been another from Jackson telling her that Everett had stopped by the bakery and left him with a message: He's ready to listen when you're ready to talk. She wasn't going to be able to stay away forever. They needed her at the bakery and the café was opening on Monday. But she was going to take this weekend for herself to figure some things out.

After a quick shower, Mariah slid into a velour jumpsuit and headed to the kitchen. She found Belinda standing over the stove, stirring contents in a pot, what looked like the makings of dinner.

"Smells good," Mariah commented.

"Thanks," she said. "It's just pasta primavera. I can manage that much. Isn't it funny that I'm a great baker, but a terrible cook?"

Mariah burst out laughing. "Cooking requires creativity and you've always struck me as being somewhat…" She couldn't find the right word without offending her cousin.

"Rigid?" Belinda offered.

Mariah laughed again. "A bit."

Belinda snorted. "You wouldn't be the first to think that way. Malik said the same thing once, but he's softened my edges. Finding someone who loves you as you are, with all your faults, is pretty spectacular."

Mariah nodded and sat down at the breakfast bar.

"How about a glass of wine?"

"Love one."

"Grab a glass." Belinda inclined her head toward the wine goblets hanging from the ceiling. "I already have a bottle open for the sauce."

Mariah reached for a glass and held it out so Belinda could fill her goblet. It was white wine, but she didn't care. She could use some relaxation and took a generous sip.

"So, you want to tell me what happened last night?"

Belinda asked as she put her own goblet to her mouth and sipped.

"Everett, EJ and I had a wonderful day yesterday," Mariah started. "And I could really see us together as a family."

"Is it a problem that he has a child already?" Belinda inquired, leaning against the counter by the stove so she could keep an eye on dinner. "Because I wouldn't have thought so."

Mariah shook her head. "Not at all. I love EJ. He's a great kid. Wonderful, actually. He calls me Miss Mariah. Can you believe that?"

"He sounds respectful."

Mariah nodded. "Then we came back to Everett's, and after EJ went to bed, we made love. And then—then he told me he loved me."

"Oh, Mariah, that's wonderful."

"I know. And I should have been happy. And I was. For all of a millisecond. Because then he said he could see us together as a family and that could give EJ a little brother or sister."

Belinda nodded. "Now I understand."

"Do you?" Mariah asked, scooting off the bar stool with her wine goblet. She walked to the floor-to-ceiling window to look out over Lake Michigan. She was silent before turning around. "Everett loves me, but he wants more children I can't give him."

"You don't know that."

"Don't I?" Mariah cried, and she couldn't help it, but tears began biting at her eyes. "I tried for three years with Rich, and even with the fertility treatments, it would never take."

"You have to tell Everett."

"And have him stay with me out of pity?" Mariah asked. "I can't!" She shook her head. "I won't do that to him."

"So instead you would deny him, deny yourself, love?" her cousin asked. "That could be a very solitary life, Mariah."

"It's what I deserve. I'm broken."

Belinda put down her wine goblet and rushed toward her, grabbing her by the shoulders. "You are not broken, Mariah. You are an incredibly warm, kind, giving woman with a lot to offer Everett and his son, but you have to tell him the truth. Don't shut him out."

Mariah clutched Belinda's hands as her cousin held her shoulders.

"You have to tell him," Belinda repeated.

Her words echoed in Mariah's head later that night as she tried to sleep. She knew Belinda was right. That she had to put all her cards on the table. And then, only then, if Everett chose to walk away, would she be able to say she'd done everything in her power to fight for what they had.

Chapter 19

Everett stopped by Lillian's on Sunday for one final inspection before their grand opening tomorrow. He was also hoping that, what, Mariah was there? He hadn't heard so much as a peep out of her since she'd run of his apartment more than twenty-four hours ago. He'd left countless messages and texts and received no response.

Was it over between them? He didn't understand any of this and it was driving him crazy.

He was reviewing the inventory log when Amber stepped into the café, carrying a large box. "Hey, boss," she said with a smile.

"Here, let me help you with that." Everett took the box out of her hands and set it on the counter.

"Thanks." Amber brushed her hands on her jeans. "So what brings you by? I could handle overseeing the equipment deliveries."

"I know." He'd just needed something to do to keep his

mind off Mariah. He looked up and found Amber studying him. "What?"

"You just look down and not your usual self."

"Have a lot on my mind." He began emptying the contents of the box onto the counter.

"Mariah?"

He glanced up from his task. "You know about us?"

Amber nodded. "Mariah and I are friends."

He turned around. "So you've heard from her?" He felt the first glimmer of hope he had all weekend.

She shook her head. "No, I haven't, but don't give up on her."

"I don't know, Amber. Mariah's not exactly being forthcoming and talking to me," he responded, "so it's hard not to think that she doesn't want to be with me and my son."

Amber touched his arm. "It's not like that, Mr. Myers."

"Call me Everett."

"Everett. There's just more to the story than you know."

"So she's shared her feelings with you?" Mariah could share them with Amber, a virtual stranger, and not with him? Her man, her lover. It boggled Everett's mind.

"She'll be back," Amber said, avoiding answering his question. "And when she does, please let her talk and tell you everything, because it won't be easy for her to do that. It's a like a raw scab, if you know what I mean."

Everett nodded. He understood that kind of pain, because that's how he'd felt when he'd opened up to her about Sara and her accident. The only difference was he'd done it, and Mariah was still keeping secrets from him. A secret Amber knew, but couldn't share with him.

"Thanks, Amber. I appreciate the insight."

"Anytime."

Now all he had to do was wait for Mariah to get back. Would she show up for the official launch of Myers Coffee Roasters café tomorrow? She would have to. It was her family's business. And when she did, Everett would be waiting, because he wanted answers. No, he needed them. He needed to know if she loved him just as much as he loved her.

"I'm surprised you asked *me* to take you to the airport," Shari said, when she arrived at Belinda's condo late Sunday evening to pick up Mariah. Belinda and Malik had a previous engagement that they couldn't cancel on short notice and had left for the evening.

"I know," Mariah said, "and I'd like to explain. Can we sit for a moment before we head out?" She motioned toward the living room, which was immaculately decorated in all white. It might look stark and cold to some, but it was Belinda's style and suited her and Malik's life.

"Sure," Shari said, joining her on the sofa.

Mariah glanced at her cousin, who looked beautiful as ever in jeans and a pullover sweater. However, since Mariah had last seen her, Shari's pregnancy had blossomed from a small baby bump to a large rounded belly. "First off, I want to apologize for how I behaved when I arrived yesterday. I was in a bad place and I completely overreacted."

"I'm listening," Shari said. Her small hands rested on her growing abdomen and Mariah had to admit she was just a little bit envious, but that was her cross to bear.

"You may not know this, but during my five-year marriage I tried for nearly three years to get pregnant," Mariah began. "I tried everything, Shari." Her voice shook as she spoke. "Fertility treatments, homeopathic remedies... I even quit working because I thought the stress was keeping me from getting pregnant. Nothing worked. And yesterday, when I saw you with the one thing I wanted most in the world, I freaked out. And I'm sorry."

Shari slowly rose from the sofa and came to sit beside Mariah, grasping her hands. "I'm sorry for you, Mariah. I had no idea that you'd gone through all of that. You've always been so close to Belinda that I didn't want to intrude. I wish I could have been there to help you through this when you were here."

Mariah patted her hand. "I wouldn't have let you. I wouldn't have let anyone, which is probably one of the reasons my marriage failed. Anyway, I just wanted to tell you that I'm truly happy for you and Grant and wish you the best."

Shari nodded. "Thank you. It means a lot coming from you, because I know how much it has cost you." The two women rose and hugged. "So how about I get you to the airport?"

"Oh, absolutely," Mariah said. "I have a man back home waiting for me, who deserves so much more than I've given him."

Mariah arrived on a red-eye on Monday morning with barely enough time to rush home, shower and change before she was due at the bakery. She would have to see Everett this morning at the ribbon-cutting ceremony for the café opening. It was going to be difficult to smile and act as if nothing was wrong when a serious discussion lay ahead of them, but she had to. They would have a talk later and she would tell him everything.

Today was not only the café's grand opening, but the debut of her Draynut at Lillian's. Mariah couldn't believe they were charging a whopping five dollars for the pastry, but Chase had been adamant about the price point. She just hoped that their customers would be willing to splurge on it, as well as purchase a high-end cup of coffee at Myers Coffee Roasters.

In the *Seattle Times*, Everett was running an ad Mariah had created to promote the new café location at Lillian's. It was also on his company's website and Facebook pages. Jackson was doing the same on their end for Lillian's. He'd already uploaded images of the Draynut on Instagram and set up a Pinterest page with all their baked goods. Mariah wasn't much into social media herself, but was glad Jack was on top of it.

"Good morning," she said, breezing into the kitchen at 6:00 a.m.

"You realize what time it is." Jackson glared at her.

"Yes," Mariah said, wrapping the apron around her waist and tying it at her neck. "And I'm sorry I'm late, but it was a long weekend."

"I certainly hope you enjoyed your jaunt to Chicago, while the rest of us here—" he glanced at Nancy and Kelsey, who they'd recruited to help out during her impromptu disappearing act "—have been slaving away."

Mariah came up behind him and rubbed his back. "I'm sorry, Jack, but it really couldn't be helped. But I'm here now and ready to dig in. Where do you need me?"

"Making your infamous Draynuts, for starters." He sighed. "I didn't want to do anything wrong and mess them up."

She smiled at her brother, hearing for the first time a bit of uncertainty in his voice. Usually Jack was so self-assured. "You couldn't. You're a great baker, Jackson."

"Not as good you, but I'm not bad." He offered her a warm smile. He never could stay mad at her for long. "So, chop, chop, the clock is ticking."

They worked in harmony for a couple hours until the hands of the clock edged toward nine, when they would open the bakery's doors. They'd settled on a later opening to ensure Mariah had enough time to bake up the Draynuts nice and fresh, while Nancy and Kelsey continued the additional pastry batches in the kitchen. Amber had arrived an hour early to ensure the café was ready for the opening.

Everything was starting to come together.

Mariah and Jackson finally stepped away from the kitchen to change, then met up again in the storefront, watching the crowd grow outside the store. There was already a line wrapped around the corner. They were just discussing it when Chase came through from the back, dressed in his usual suit and tie. He wasn't alone.

"Look who I found hanging outside the back door," he said. Everett stood in the doorway behind him, wearing a charcoal suit.

Mariah's pulse skittered at an alarming rate and a lump formed in her throat as she gazed at him. Outwardly he looked the same, that vital man who had captivated her from the very first time she saw him. But his eyes... Looking at his eyes, Mariah could see that a light had gone out. Had she done that to him? She hadn't meant to, but she'd been struggling so hard with her own insecurities that she hadn't been able to voice them to him.

Did he think it was his fault? That he'd done something wrong?

It wasn't; it was her. She was damaged. And she needed to tell him that.

"There was a line out there," Everett was saying, cutting into her thoughts, "so I had to park in the back and come in the rear." His eyes never left Mariah's as he spoke. They were silently pleading with her for answers. Answers that couldn't come now, but would soon.

Soon she would tell him.

"Your ad and my leak must have done it," Jackson said. He'd leaked word of the Draynut on their social media sites yesterday, hoping to generate some buzz. Clearly, it had worked.

"I took the liberty of sending a few folks from my team to divide the crowd from the press. I thought we'd let the media in first so we could capture the grand opening," Everett said. "Hope that's all right?"

"That was quick thinking," Chase replied evenly. "Thanks, Myers."

"No problem."

Chase bumped Mariah's hip as he came toward her, startling her out of daydreaming about Everett. "Excited?"

She forced a smile. "Heck, yeah. I just hope the Draynut lives up to our high expectations."

"It will, it will, sis," Chase said. "You've created a winner."

"Thanks, Chase." She hazarded a glance at Everett, but he was already walking toward the café. Dear Lord! She hadn't even checked in on Amber. Mariah sighed heavily She really was failing on all fronts.

"Everything okay over here?" Everett asked Amber after he'd opened the front door and allowed members of the press in to set up. Several local newspeople had arrived for the ribbon cutting ceremony for Myers Coffee Roasters café and the Draynut's debut.

As much as he craved to talk to Mariah and find out exactly what was going on with her, he also wanted to ensure the opening went off without a hitch. He knew he didn't have to worry; Amber was not only an expert barista, but a seasoned manager able to oversee operations. However, Everett liked being hands-on.

It was why he'd limited his cafés to the Seattle market. Not only had he always wanted to be available, but he'd wanted to be able to stop in and check in on business whenever the mood struck him, just as his father had with the hotels. And look how well it had served him!

Nonetheless, Everett was here now and would roll up his sleeves and get dirty if needed. But apparently he didn't need to, because everything was in order. The displays were stocked with Myers Coffee Roaster beans, as well as ground coffee and carry mugs for purchase. The menu boards mounted on the wall proudly displayed their signature coffee selections.

"I have it all under control," Amber was saying.

"Of course you do." He eyed his bohemian barista, who was decked in the standard Myers Coffee Roasters black shirt over a flowing blue skirt, with some chunky jewelry on her wrists and around her neck. Her hair was signature Amber in tight curls that hung to her shoulders. "I have the best staff."

"Thanks, boss—Everett." Amber smiled brightly. "We'll make you proud."

"Well, then let's open this place," Everett said as he stepped back over the threshold into Lillian's bakery section. "We're a go here!" he yelled across the room. He avoided looking at Mariah, which was hard, considering she'd looked spectacular in a black-and-white pleated skirt and simple red keyhole top.

He'd nearly stumbled when he'd seen her standing beside her brother when he'd come in. He'd known she wouldn't miss the launch, but was business the only reason she'd come back?

Had she come back for him?

The clock chimed nine, signaling it was time to start, and Mariah watched Chase open the doors to let the general public in. Soon, customers were filing into their small establishment.

As she stood at the register, Mariah was surprised at just how many people had come out. They had a steady stream of customers, and she and Jackson were handling them easily until a reporter asked to interview her about her concept for the Draynut.

Chase came over to the register, allowing Mariah to join the newswoman, who was just finishing an interview with Everett.

The reporter, a fresh-faced Asian woman, turned to her and said, "Mr. Myers was just telling us that you two worked closely on the concept for the café."

Mariah glanced over at Everett through hooded lashes. Of course he would give her part of the credit, when he'd come up with the whole idea in the first place. But that's who Everett was—a kind and giving man.

"Yes, we did," Mariah said, smiling into the camera. "It's been a great partnership."

"And the Draynut?" the reporter asked. "Looks like it's a hit with the locals." The camera turned to pan the bakery, which still had a lineup an hour after opening. "How did you come up with the idea?"

Mariah answered all her questions, but her mind was still on Everett, who'd quietly left the interview area.

"I think we have it," the reporter finally said, interrupting her thoughts. "Thank you."

"No, thank *you*." Mariah shook her hand.

She was about to search for Everett when Jackson called out to her, "We need more Draynuts."

"I'm on it," Mariah replied, heading toward the kitchen. Her conversation would have to wait.

It was nearly two hours after opening that the line at the bakery slowed down and Mariah and her brothers had a chance to breathe. They left Kelsey in the storefront to deal with customers while they went to the kitchen.

Once away from the public, Jackson held out his palm. "High five! High five!" he yelled, slapping his siblings' hands "Was that not an incredible day or what?"

"I can't believe it, either!" Mariah clasped both hands to her cheeks. "We sold out of every Draynut and have orders for tomorrow."

"We did it!" Chase pumped his fist in excitement. "The Draynut is on the map and that was a great start." He leaned against the kitchen counter. "And very encouraging, but we have to think about how we can keep the momentum going."

"C'mon, Chase," Jackson said. "Can't we enjoy our success for a minute before we have to think about the bottom line?"

Mariah nodded. "I'm with Jack on this one. This was no easy feat, so let's just enjoy today and think about strategy tomorrow."

Chase shrugged. "If that's how you guys feel, then I'll defer to you both. But we can't rest on our laurels too long, because Sweetness Bakery is an institution just like Myers Coffee Roasters." He pointed toward the café, which still had a small line. "And we have our work cut out for us if we intend to overtake them."

"I agree with you," Mariah said. "But I have a few things I'm working on. I spent years perfecting the Draynut recipe. So all that time I was at home, and you all thought I had nothing but babies on the brain, I was working."

Jackson walked over and kissed her on the cheek. "We couldn't thank you enough, sis. And I'll be right here with you, trying to find the next best thing."

"Then let's celebrate," Chase said. He headed to the large commercial refrigerator and pulled out a bottle of champagne.

"When did you get that?" Mariah asked.

"Yesterday," he answered, "because I knew we had a winner on our hands. Get some cups," he said, as he popped the cork.

Jackson and Mariah rushed over with red plastic cups before the champagne could spill on the floor.

"Can we get in on this celebration or is it just for family?" Everett asked from the doorway, with Amber standing behind him.

Mariah warmed inwardly when she saw her man. "C'mon in," she said, laughing, "We couldn't have done this without you."

She handed her cup to Amber, then reached for more for herself, Everett and Nancy and Kelsey. When they all had champagne, Chase toasted, "To teamwork!"

"To teamwork!" they all shouted in unison.

Everett placed his cup in a nearby trash can. "Well, as much as I'd love to stay, I have to get to the office. But I just want to say great job to everyone. I'm looking forward to our collaboration here."

"So are we." Chase walked over to him and shook his hand.

Everett started toward the back door, where he was parked, but was stopped by a hand on his arm. He felt a spark of electricity. It was Mariah. He spun around to face her.

"Can we talk?" she asked. Her face was flushed from the craziness of the last few hours and there was an an almost imperceptible note of pleading in her face. A face he'd come to love, but which in the last couple days had caused him such heartache.

Everett shook his head. "Now isn't a good time. I have to get to work."

She eyed him suspiciously, as if she didn't believe him,

but said, "All right. Then later? I could come over to your place?"

He nodded. "That's fine."

He watched her shoulders visibly sag in relief, as if she'd thought he would say otherwise. He wouldn't do that to her or to him. They did have to talk, but without an audience and when they had plenty of time.

And now wasn't it.

"What time?" Mariah inquired.

"After 7:00 p.m."

"I'll be there."

Everett nodded and headed toward the door. It was so hard to walk away from Mariah, when all he really wanted to do was pull her in his arms and kiss her until the ache went away. But he couldn't, not until she was honest and bared her heart to him, as he'd done. Until she did, there was no hope for a future together.

Chapter 20

Mariah was nervous as she made her way to Everett's. Earlier, when she'd tried to speak to him, his implacable expression had been unnerving. She had no idea what his mood would be. It had been nearly seventy-two hours since she'd walked out of his bedroom in the middle of the night after he'd told her he loved her. She'd wanted to tell him she loved him just as much, but she'd been too scared. And now, she risked losing him because of her fear of getting hurt again. She just prayed it wasn't too late.

After a quick stop home to shower and change into a velour jumpsuit, she made it to his penthouse exactly at 7:00 p.m., as he'd requested. Her legs felt wooden as she approached his door.

Everett opened it wearing drawstring sweats and a dark T-shirt. "Hey." He gave her a tentative smile. "Come on in."

Mariah stepped inside and felt as if she was walking on eggshells, unsure of what to do next. Everett certainly wasn't making it any easier, because he didn't greet her with a kiss.

The apartment was quiet save for some jazz music playing softly in the background. "Where's EJ?" she inquired as she followed Everett into the kitchen.

"With my parents," he responded, pulling two wine goblets out of the cabinets. "I thought it best that we have some privacy. Wouldn't you agree?"

She nodded as a lump formed in her throat.

"Wine?" he asked, holding up a bottle that had already been uncorked.

"Yes," she managed to squeak. She supposed some liquid courage wouldn't hurt.

He poured each of them a glass of wine and handed her one before heading toward the living room. She followed him to the sofa. He sat far away from her on one side, so she took his cue and settled opposite him. He leaned back against the cushions and crossed one leg over the other.

Mariah turned to face him and found he was studying her quietly, waiting for her to speak.

She cleared her throat and then took a sip of the delicious vintage before placing her goblet on the cocktail table in front of them. She clasped her hands nervously together in her lap. Apparently, he wasn't going to make this any easier for her, so she was going to have to speak.

"I'm sorry about the other night," Mariah began. "I shouldn't have run out and left you like that."

He sipped his wine. "No, you shouldn't have. You left me without an explanation, leaving me to wonder what it all meant. So tell me, Mariah, what does it mean?"

She swallowed. "It means I'm scared."

"Why?" He sat up and placed his goblet next to hers. "Have I done something wrong?"

She shook her head. "No. No, you didn't. You did everything right. Just as you've always done. You've been patient with me, kind, giving, loving…" Her voice trailed off.

"Then why? Why would you leave me?"

Mariah heard the accusatory tone in Everett's voice and knew that she'd hurt him terribly. She gulped and hot tears began spilling down her cheeks. She shook her head. "I was scared. Scared that you would leave me once you found out."

"Find out what?" Everett asked. "Jesus, Mariah! Don't you know that there's nothing you could ever say that would change my feelings for you? I want to marry you," he blurted out. "I want you to be EJ's mom and my wife."

"What?" Had he really just said he wanted to marry her?

He smiled softly. "You heard me. I said I want to marry you. And I think you want to marry me, too, but there's something holding you back. What is it? You have to talk to me, baby."

Mariah wished she could say yes to his marriage proposal with no reservations, but she had to tell him her predicament. "I can't, because you have to know that I…" She flushed with embarrassment and her cheeks burned at having to tell Everett the secret she'd held on to that had been her shame for years. Gulping, she gazed at him in despair. "I may not be able to have children."

"What?" Everett left his spot and immediately scooted closer to her on the couch. His large hands grasped hers. "What do you mean?"

"I could be infertile."

A deep frown etched Everett's forehead. "How do you know? Have you been tested?"

Mariah nodded. "I've been poked and prodded every which way but Sunday." She attempted a laugh, but instead it turned into a sob, and that's when Everett's arms encircled her, pulling her close. He gently rocked her back and forth as she buried her burning face in his shoulder and wept.

When she began to calm, she lifted her head to meet his searching eyes, "My quest to get pregnant broke up my first marriage. I quit my job so I could try fertility treatments and homeopathic remedies, but nothing worked. I tried for three years to conceive. The stress and strain was too much for our young marriage and he began to resent me, until eventually we drifted apart. I don't want that to happen to you and me. If it did, I—I wouldn't survive."

"So instead you ran?" Everett asked, searching her face. Hearing Mariah's confession was a surprise, of course, yet it explained so much. Her reluctance to date him so soon after her divorce, and why she'd run the other night when he'd told her he loved her and had brought up having more children.

Mariah nodded. "I was scared, and then you told me you loved me and it was all just too much."

"Listen, baby…" He reached for her hand. "I am so sorry for all the pain you endured, trying to have a child. I don't care if you can't have kids." He paused and then corrected himself, "Well, that's not exactly true. I do want more kids. But I won't put you through that again. That would be your choice. If we're just meant to be a family of three, I'll be fine with that. Or maybe someday you might consider adopting?"

He couldn't lose Mariah. He loved her too much and he would do anything for her, because that's what you did when you truly loved someone. You made sacrifices and risks for those you loved.

* * *

Mariah stared back at Everett, dumbstruck. He would be willing to adopt? After her ex-husband, she'd thought that wouldn't be an option for most men, but then again, Everett wasn't your average man. He was better. And he was hers. "Do you really mean that? You'd be willing to have other children even if they weren't yours?"

"Of course I would."

"I—I'm floored," Mariah admitted. It was beyond anything she had ever expected. "I never thought you'd consider adoption. I know how proud you are of EJ, and so many men have a thing about passing on their heritage. Are you sure, Everett? There are so many women out there who could give you your own biological child. *Children.*"

"There is no one out there who can give me what I want, because that's you. Besides which, we could hire a surrogate, perhaps, to carry our biological child. Whatever you want, sweetheart. We have options."

"And what about Sara?" Mariah knew it was silly to bring his deceased wife up at a time like this, but she had to get all her fears, all her issues, on the table and lay them bare.

He frowned. "What about her?"

"I just know how much you loved her, and you still live here…"

"That's true, but I firmly believe you can have more than one great love in a lifetime. Mariah, I love you," Everett continued. "I love you for you, not for what you can give me, or to help me get over my dead wife. I love *you.*"

Everett loved her so much that he was willing to forgo having another child? He'd adopt or agree to surrogacy? This wonderful, incredible man loved her. And Mariah finally believed it. Her heart soared with joy and she clutched both sides of his face, finally saying what had been in her heart for weeks. "And I love you, too, Everett. I love you with all my heart."

"You do?" His voice rose with joy, as if he was surprised to hear her say so.

She nodded as tears slid down her face. "I do." She kissed his cheeks, one at a time, before coming to his mouth and brushing her lips across his. In seconds, Everett's arms was encircling her waist and pulling her forward as he deepened the kiss.

He dropped backward on the couch and she fell atop him happily as they hungrily kissed as if they were starved for the taste of each other. They wildly touched and caressed, and it didn't take long for clothes to start flying across the room and landing on the floor, they were both so desperate to get closer and join as one. Their bodies felt so good, so right, so made for each other.

Once they were naked, Everett reached down between them to make sure she was ready for him. Mariah's breasts turned to hardened points. She was so hot and wet for him, just as she always was whenever they were together. That didn't stop Everett from stroking her core. She tried clenching her thighs, to brace herself for what was to come, but he was having none of it and spread her legs apart to accommodate his searching fingers.

He stroked her damp, trembling sex with one finger and then two, thrusting deep inside her. Mariah felt every pulse-pounding increment of time as he teased her swollen flesh. She clutched at the fabric of the couch as he continued to kiss her passionately, before nuzzling his lips against her cheek, her neck. His breath gusted hard and hot against her ear. When she began to shudder beneath his fingers, Everett removed his hand and instead of settling himself between her thighs, leaned backward on the couch so Mariah could ride him.

She slid on top of his already throbbing manhood. "Everett," she moaned, as she impaled herself atop him. Slowly, he began rolling underneath her. Having him inside her, moving slowly, rhythmically, was so intense Mariah knew it was just a matter of time before another climax would hit, just as strong as the first.

"Jesus," Everett groaned beneath her, "I love you so much, Mariah."

"I love you, too," she cried as she undulated against him. Everett was stirring her into a frenzy and she could feel the pressure of another orgasm coming.

Everett continued to urge her on, clutching her bare bottom as he helped her slide up and down his hardened shaft. "Yes, like that, Mariah." His breathing was becoming ragged and the sounds he made caused excitement to ripple through her. "Like that, sweet angel."

He knew how to find her sexual peak and greedily give her every part of himself, and Mariah knew she would never tire of having him buried to the hilt inside her. She loved this man and would love him to her dying day. That he was willing to make adjustments for them to expand their family told her just how lucky she was to have Everett and EJ in her life.

When Everett flipped her over onto her back and began pounding into her quivering flesh, Mariah heard herself scream and Everett roar as both their bodies erupted. She clutched him to her breasts and whispered over and over, "Everett, Everett, Everett…"

Chapter 21

Early the next morning, Mariah and Everett rolled out of bed much earlier than she would have liked. Last night they'd finally made their way to his bedroom after they'd christened every inch of his penthouse, from the couch to the floor to the kitchen countertop to the terrace outside. There was no place he hadn't taken her, and Mariah had loved every minute of it, just as much as she loved the man himself.

They'd come up for air and showered early so they could head to Everett's parents' home to pick up EJ and take him to school that morning. Everett was excited to tell him the news.

"Are you sure he's going to be happy about this?" Mariah asked in the SUV. Although they had shared an amazing day at the wildlife park and spent some evenings together, she and Everett had fallen in love rather quickly, in barely two months, and she wasn't sure that was enough time for EJ to catch up with his feelings toward her.

"Yes, I'm sure," Everett responded, squeezing her hand. "EJ adores you."

Mariah sure hoped so.

When they arrived, his parents and EJ were sitting at the kitchen table. Based on the plates and cutlery, it looked as if they'd just finished breakfast. EJ was already dressed for school in chinos and a polo shirt.

"Hey, Mom, Dad," Everett said as he reached for Mariah's hand. "I have some news."

"Morning, son." His father nodded over his morning cup of coffee. "Mariah." He smiled warmly at her. "It's good to see you again."

"You as well," she replied. "Mrs. Myers." She smiled at his mother, who looked questioningly at the two of them, given the time of day.

"Dad!" EJ rushed toward him, nearly tackling him to the ground. He noticed that Everett didn't release Mariah's hand, and he glanced up at the two of them. "What's going on? Are you both here to take me to school?"

Everett gave Mariah a sideways glance and she nodded in approval. "We're here because I asked Mariah to marry me and she said yes."

"What?" Shock was evident on his mother's face. "Really? So soon?"

"Yes, really, Mom." A grin spread across Everett's face.

"Congratulations, son, that's great news." His father rose to offer his hand, which Everett enthusiastically pumped.

"Thanks, we're really happy," he said, and then bent to look down at his son. "But I'm hoping someone else is happy about our news."

Mariah watched the exchange between father and son. "How do you feel about it, EJ? About having Mariah as your mom?"

EJ's curly head looked up at Mariah, so she, too, crouched lower so she could face him. She knew what a big deal this was. It had been EJ and his father for the last five years, and this would be a big change, having her in his life, sharing his father's time. EJ's response would set the tone for their relationship and could potentially end their short engagement before it had begun.

"I know this is kind of sudden for you," Mariah said to EJ, "but I'm hoping that I can spend my life with you and your dad, if you'll let me. Because I love him..." She glanced at Everett, who had tears in his eyes. "And—and you." Her voice trembled, but she continued on because she had more to say. "I—I know you already had a mother and I wouldn't dream of replacing her, but I'm hoping that in time you'll let me in because I'd love to be your mom. If you want me."

EJ surprised her by rushing toward her and wrapping his small arms around her neck. "Omigod!" Her heart welled with love and tears streamed down her cheeks. That tiny action had touched her heart more than he would ever know, and she hugged him back with all her might.

Everett came toward them and wrapped his arms around the two of them. "I love you both, and we're a family now."

Mariah glanced up at him. "That's right. Forever and always."

* * * * *

REQUEST YOUR FREE BOOKS!

2 FREE NOVELS
PLUS 2 FREE GIFTS!

KIMANI™ ROMANCE

Love's ultimate destination!